ROBOTS GO WILD!

For more information about James Patterson's novels, visit
www.jamespatterson.co.uk

HOUSE OF ROBOTS

ROBOTS GO WILD!

JAMES PATTERSON
AND CHRIS GRABENSTEIN

ILLUSTRATED BY JULIANA NEUFELD

1 3 5 7 9 10 8 6 4 2

Young Arrow
20 Vauxhall Bridge Road
London SW1V 2SA

Young Arrow is part of the Penguin Random House group of companies
whose addresses can be found at global.penguinrandomhouse.com

Penguin
Random House
UK

Copyright © James Patterson 2015
Illustrations by Juliana Neufeld
Excerpt from *House of Robots* copyright © James Patterson 2014
Illustrations in excerpt by Juliana Neufeld

First published by Young Arrow in 2015

www.randomhouse.co.uk

A CIP catalogue record for this book
is available from the British Library

Hardback ISBN 9780099568292
Trade paperback ISBN 9780099568322

Printed and bound by Clays Ltd, St Ives Plc

ROBOTS GO WILD!

CHAPTER 1

Hi! I'm Sammy Hayes-Rodriguez, and if you have trouble crawling out of bed on school days, you should do what I do: live with robots!

That's right. Our whole house is filled with whirring, whizzing, rumbling, rambling robots—all of them designed by my mother. Mom's not exactly a mad scientist, but she comes pretty close.

She invented one bot named Buzz whose only job is to zip into my bedroom at exactly seven o'clock every morning, hover around my bed, and make loud, annoying noises. If you try to bop his snooze button (his little red hat), Buzz's motion detectors will sense your hand movement, and he'll scoot sideways. You'll be slapping air, and he'll keep making irritating noises until your feet finally hit the floor.

This is why I'm usually awake by 7:01.

Even my closet and chest of drawers are semi-robotic. Prepackaged sets of underwear and socks pop up the instant I tug open a drawer. The closet, which is linked to outdoor weather-reporting devices, knows what shirt, sweater, or hoodie I should wear. It's also equipped with a pants sniffer and can fling me my cleanest pair of jeans.

Why the big, robotic rush to get to school on time?

Mostly it's for my little sister, Maddie.

She's in the third grade, and trust me, there has never, ever been a kid more excited about going to school than Maddie Hayes-Rodriguez. On school days, she acts the way most kids do on snow days.

Like me, all the robots bopping around our house absolutely adore Maddie and treat her like a princess. Especially Geoffrey, the brand-new butler-bot. Mom gave him a British accent, so he sounds a little snooty.

"Good morning, children," he says to Maddie and me. "Breakfast is served."

The second he says that, the Breakfastinator—one of Mom's wackiest automated cooking contraptions—hurls a few slices of French toast at us like it's making a serve in volleyball. The machine also tosses over a couple tubs of syrup and chucks us some butter pats. You do not want to be here when the Breakfastinator serves up biscuits and gravy.

DING!

WOOSH

THWACK!

READY

THIS IS UNACCEPTABLE BEHAVIOR. IT IS ALSO UNACCEPTABLE BUTTER BECAUSE IT WAS ON THE FLOOR LONGER THAN 3 SECONDS.

If Maddie needs anything—anything at all—Mom's robots spring into action.

If her pencil needs sharpening, McFetch, the robotic dog, will gnaw it down to a perfect point.

If she needs help with her homework, Tootles the tut-bot—a retro, rolling tutor computer—will point her in the right direction.

If she needs an after-school snack, the Breakfastinator will fling fruit at her.

As you can probably tell, my little sister is different from most kids her age.

For one thing, she's awesome.

For another, even though she's in the third grade, she only started going to school for the first time a month ago, after the school year had already started for most kids.

I'll explain later. Promise.

But first, you've got to meet E.

He's my bro-bot.

CHAPTER 2

This is E.

When Mom first created him and said I had to take a robot to school with me every day, I thought E stood for *Error*—as in the biggest, hugest, most colossal mistake ever made. And, at first, he *did* make my life at school pretty nutso.

But then I found out why E had such enormous blue eyes.

ROBOTS TAKE THE BEST SELFIES. THEIR ARMS ARE **SUPER** EXTENDABLE.

Oh, right. Duh. The drawing is in black and white. But trust me, E's eyes are Blizzard Blue. The exact same color as Maddie's.

See, Mom created E (she says the E stands for *Egghead*) to be Maddie's eyes, ears, and voice in Ms. Tracey's third-grade classroom at Creekside Elementary.

Why doesn't Maddie just go to school herself?

She can't. Not without getting really sick.

Now, I know a lot kids say going to school makes them sick. Especially on days when the cafeteria special is the beefy-cheesy nacho surprise.

But just going to school and breathing the air and being near other kids and all their germs could make my little sister seriously ill, because Maddie suffers from SCID, which is short for *severe combined immunodeficiency*. Basically, it means Maddie's body has a really hard time fighting off any kind of infection. If somebody coughs and forgets to cover their mouth, she could wind up in the hospital.

So what does it all mean? Well, Maddie hardly ever leaves home. In fact, she hardly ever leaves her room. That's why our family pet is a germ-free robot dog.

Why Mr. Moppenshine, the multiarmed multitasker, is constantly cleaning and disinfecting everything.

It's also why the only way for Maddie to actually go to school is for E to go there for her.

"You'd better hurry up, you guys! You don't want to be late."

That's my dad. Noah Rodriguez, the world-famous graphic novelist. He works from home, so he's never late.

"Your father is correct," says E. "We must not tarry."

Yep. E still sounds a little robot-ish. But he can't help it. Mom made him that way. Guess what she's making next? I'm not 100 percent sure, but I think it'll help Mr. Moppenshine scrub the toilets.

"Let's go, Sammy."

That's Maddie, speaking through E, just like she'll do at school. When the first bell rings, Maddie will run E from the nifty control pod set up in her room.

I just hope she doesn't make E do something super girly, like scream about boy bands or spin like a ballerina.

At least, not while I'm around.

CHAPTER 3

Oops.

I think E and I are going to be a little tardy for school today.

When we step out the back door and hurry down the steps—something, by the way, that E does incredibly well for a robot—there's a whole mob of people waiting for us in the driveway.

I guess word has spread about what E's been doing for Maddie at the elementary school.

A few faces in the crowd are familiar. I recognize the ones who teach or work at Notre Dame, the university where Mom is a professor of computer science in the College of Engineering. I also see star reporters from the South Bend, Indiana, TV news shows. The people I've never seen before are mostly wearing suits and ties.

Mom, of course, is there, in her lab coat, beaming proudly.

"Eggy, why don't you show these folks some of your moves?" she suggests.

"My pleasure," says E.

He moonwalks across the driveway to the garage, where my dad hung a basketball hoop.

"Feed me the b-ball, Sammy," says E. "Bounce me the rock. Distribute the basketball."

Yup. I taught E every bit of basketball slang I know.

I toss him the ball. He twirls around and makes a high-arcing shot.

E snags the ball as it bounces off the back-board, and he lands with a hydraulic, knee-bending *FLOOSH, FLISH, FWUMP.* Then he springs back up, like he has rockets in his heels, and—*WHOOSH... THUNK!*—tomahawk-dunks the ball.

The crowd goes wild.

"But wait, there's more!" says E, sounding like

a late-night TV infomercial. "With Maddie's help, I can also spell all of this week's vocabulary words. For instance, *flutter*. F-L-U-T-T-E-R. Now I will use it in a sentence. 'My butter will flutter over my toast.' Speaking of toast, I can also make toaster tarts for a tasty after-school treat."

You guessed it. Warm pastry topped with swirly icing shoots out of his ears.

"Dr. Hayes," says a roly-poly man with a belly that's about to pop a button on his shirt, "your creation is magnificent."

"Thank you, Mr. Riley."

Oooh. I've heard Mom and Dad talk about Mr. Max Riley at the dinner table before. From what I picked up between bites of mac and cheese, Mr. Riley is a very important, very wealthy graduate of Notre Dame who gives a lot of money to his old school.

I AM DELIGHTED TO SEE ALL MY MONEY BEING PUT TO SUCH GOOD USE. NOW, PERHAPS YOU CAN GIVE THE NOTRE DAME FOOTBALL AND BASKETBALL TEAMS SIMILAR JUMPING TECHNOLOGY?

"As the largest contributor to the College of Engineering," Mr. Riley continues, "let me just say that this is a great day for Notre Dame! And, if I may quote legendary author Kurt Vonnegut, 'Science is magic that works.'

"So three cheers for Professor Elizabeth Hayes and her magical robotic creation, E, the substitute student!"

As a dozen people start singing the "cheer, cheer" part of the Notre Dame fight song, E and I climb aboard our bikes.

We pedal away, stirring up a wake of swirling autumn leaves, and E can't resist showing off all sorts of bike stunts he learned when Mom slipped a *BMX-treme* DVD into his internal disk drive.

CHAPTER 4

On our way to school, E and I are joined by my second-best friend since forever, good ol' Triple H himself, Harry Hunter Hudson.

Everyone just calls him Trip.

See how banged up Trip's bike is? Not to be mean or anything, but Trip is kind of a klutz. He bumps into stuff *all the time.* Once, he crashed his bike into a park bench he thought was making a right turn.

When Trip's not bumbling, fumbling,

Hi, Guys! SORRY IT TOOK ME SO LONG TO GET HERE. THREE WHOLE CHAPTERS!

or dropping heavy objects on his own foot, he's usually saying exactly the wrong thing at the wrong time. Like once, at the zoo, he said, "Are you going to eat that?"

To a tiger.

Speaking of food, Trip packs peanut-butter-and-banana sandwiches for lunch every day. Nothing else. Not even a plain banana or a pack of peanut butter crackers. It's PB&Bs Monday through Friday. Weekends, too. (I've had lunch at his house. His mom buys bananas in those gigantic bunches you see on banana trees.)

Some kids at Creekside Elementary make fun of Trip and his goofy clothes and his goofier dinosaur backpack and his stinky peanut-butter-and-banana breath and his crazy klutziness, but I don't. I think hanging with him is fun.

And always interesting.

Trip and I have been second-besties since kindergarten, back when he used to dip his PB&Bs in a jar of library paste.

Having a friend like Trip doesn't exactly make you super popular in school.

But then E came along. Now everybody wants to hang with us because they think E is super-cool.

That's why, lately, Trip is so excited about school.

"These have been the best two weeks of my whole entire life," he tells me. "Even counting Disney World."

Trip says he's packed an extra peanut-butter-and-banana sandwich in his lunch box.

"It's for E. If he eats it, nobody will think I'm weird anymore, because everything E does is so awesomely cool."

"Um, E doesn't eat food," I remind Trip.

"So? He can pretend. He could hide it in his mouth hole."

"Not really. The sandwich would just gum up the speakers in there."

E reminds us both that his "primary objective" is to function as Maddie's eyes, ears, and mouth in Ms. Tracey's third-grade classroom.

"I am sorry, Trip, but I cannot have bread, peanut butter, or bananas interfering with my mission."

"That's right," says Maddie, her voice coming out of E's mouth, which, if it had one of Trip's sticky peanut-butter-and-banana sandwiches mashed up inside, would sound more like "Mrats mright."

"By the way," Maddie continues, "I was just watching the morning news in my room."

I can hear the smile in Maddie's voice.

"And?" I ask.

"Be prepared," she says with a giggle. "You boys are in for a *huge* surprise. Maddie out."

CHAPTER 5

All righty-o.

I guess this is our surprise: a humongous traffic jam in the drop-off lane at school where everybody has lined up to greet Trip, me, and—oh yeah, I nearly forgot—E!

The drop-off lane is mobbed. Horns are honking. Parents are furious.

All because of E.

It is absolutely *awesome*!

"Dismount, fellows," says E. "According to the rules of safe bicycling, we should always walk our bikes through any busy intersections."

"This isn't an intersection," says Trip. "It's a parking lot! Eeh-eeh-eeh."

Did I mention that Trip laughs backward? When he does, he sounds like a mule with asthma.

"Excuse me," says E as we walk our rides over to the bike racks. "Passing on your left." Then he makes a *DINKLE-TINKLE-DINK-DINK* noise like a bike bell.

The crowd parts.

All the kids who go to Creekside, plus the teachers and Mrs. Reyes, the principal, are lined up on the sidewalk leading to the front door.

E gives them a slow and steady "window washer" wave.

Almost everybody is clapping and cheering. Some kids have even painted banners.

Trip is eating it up. "This is better than a peanut-butter-and-banana sandwich with extra bananas!"

O-kay. I hope he never brings one of *those* to school.

The guys from the local news stations zoom in on us and beam our image via satellite back to their live broadcasts.

Even though 99.9 percent of everybody *loves* E, I'm also picking up some angry glares and annoyed sighs from Penelope Pettigrew, a girl in Maddie's third-grade class.

I don't mind her being mean to me; she's just a bratty little kid I usually ignore. But I get totally steamed when she starts making fun of Maddie.

Fortunately, E doesn't like it, either.

CHAPTER 6

I'll escort your little 'sister' to Ms. Tracey's classroom," Penelope says after we're inside the school building.

She grabs for E's arm.

I block her. "Um, that's okay. I promised my mom and dad that I'd walk E, er, Maddie to her classroom every morning."

Penelope pouts and jabs a hand to her hip. "But I'm going there *anyway*!" She gives me a major eye roll. Penelope Pettigrew can make anything and everything sound *sooooo* dramatic.

"Thanks for the offer," I tell her, "but I promised."

Penelope rolls her eyes. Again. She rolls them so often, I think maybe she likes looking up into her own brain.

I CAN ROLL MY EYEBALLS, TOO. BUT USUALLY I TAKE THEM OUT OF MY HEAD FIRST.

"Fine," Penelope huffs. "Take 'Maddie' to class. What*ever*. See if I care. But your *sister* the robot cannot sit in the front row anymore. She blocks everybody's view. Plus, she smells like toaster tarts. YUCK!"

"Pardon me, Penelope," says E, "but I will sit wherever Ms. Tracey instructs me to sit, as is proper third-grade etiquette. But thank you for your concern. Would you like a toaster tart?"

Now she sighs, closes her eyes, and makes a stink face. "You are *soooo* gross."

She stomps off to Ms. Tracey's room.

"Come on, E," I say. "The bell's about to ring." I turn to Trip because he and I are in the same class. "Save me a seat."

"How about the one next to mine?"

"Yeah."

"No problemo. Nobody else ever wants to sit there anyway."

Trip heads off to our classroom while E and I hustle down the hall through a swarm of first, second, and third graders, most of whom want to fist-bump with me and E. I glance at my watch.

In exactly one minute, Maddie will take over complete control of our bro-bot.

From the doorway to her classroom, I ask Ms. Tracey where she would like "Maddie" to sit.

"Up front like always," says Ms. Tracey with a smile. "We don't want anything blocking her view of the Smart Board."

"OMG," I hear Penelope mutter under her breath. "Total teacher's pet."

"Thanks for the official escort," says Maddie from inside E. "I'll take it from here."

We say our good-byes, and Maddie expertly marches E down the rows of desks. His hydraulic legs are *ZHURR-CLICK-ZHURR*ing perfectly. Most of the kids in the classroom, the ones who aren't Penelope Pettigrew, smile and wave at E—I mean Maddie.

"Hi, Maddie," they say.

"Hi, guys," Maddie says through E. "Who wants to play basketball at recess with me today?"

All the hands (except one, of course) shoot up.

"Me!"

"I do!"

"Will you boost me up so I can dunk again?"

"You bet!" says Maddie as E takes his seat in the first row of desks.

The bell rings, and even though I should be running down the hall to my own classroom, I hang in the doorway for a few seconds. It's so cool that Maddie has so many new friends, thanks to E.

He really is Mom's best invention ever.

Well, that's what I'm thinking today.

By the end of next week?

Not so much.

CHAPTER 7

During the school day, while Maddie is in Ms. Tracey's class, Trip and I are down the hall in Mrs. Kunkel's room.

Up until a few days ago, E used to sit in *my* class so Mom could beta test her bot for Maddie.

SIGH...

E SAT HERE

See those frowns on our faces? We both miss E, big-time.

Sure, he used to be sort of goofy and was always trying to spell *Kyrgyzstan*—even when nobody asked him to—but he was also fun.

Mrs. Kunkel tells us to open our books and read silently while she goes down to the principal's office "for a quick minute" to check in with Mrs. Reyes about something. Principal Reyes is a friend of Mom's. They even play together in a rock band called Almost Pretty Bad. Personally, I think they should change their name to Awfully Loud, because they're pretty awful. And loud about it, too.

Anyway, the second Mrs. Kunkel's gone, Jacob Gorski, who's president of the Creekside Robotics Club, switches on his latest contraption and, thumbing its remote control, sends the chunky toy robot across the room to me.

It takes *forever.*

I half expect the thing's batteries to die before it finally slogs its way up two desks and over three.

When it finally bumps into the leg of my chair and topples over onto its side (with its legs still chug-chug-chugging away), I notice that Gorski's plastic-brick

bot has a note taped to its blocky arm; unlike E, Gorski's homemade robot doesn't have any kind of pinchers.

I tug the note free and read what Gorski has written:

Great.

Gorski's calling me the name that my worst enemy in the known universe, Cooper Elliot, used to call me: "Dweebiac."

Cooper doesn't go to Creekside anymore. He sort of got expelled for robo-napping E back in September. Now that it's the middle of October, I guess Jacob Gorski has decided he's going to take Cooper Elliot's place.

Yep. I may have lost a robot, but I've gained a new, nerdier bully.

CHAPTER 8

Maddie (that is, E) is now the most popular kid at Creekside Elementary.

Ever. And the school's been here in South Bend, Indiana, for decades. It's even older than my parents, who are ancient. They're both way over thirty.

THANKS, MADDIE! I CAN SEE MY HOUSE FROM UP HERE!

SLAM!

Not only is Maddie fantastic fun during recess, but on rainy days her remote-controlled robot can wirelessly beam movies from his memory chips to the classroom's Smart Board. Maddie always makes sure that E has a wide assortment of Pixar titles loaded onto his hard drive. And *Frozen*. Third graders could watch *Frozen* over and over for a week. They like singing that song. Over and over and over.

What makes E/Maddie more popular than ever is the fact that now he (or, I guess, she) doesn't talk like a robot. From eight to three, Monday through Friday, the robot talks and laughs and giggles like a normal third-grade girl. During school hours, E *is* Maddie. Together, they both just auditioned for the school choir. They also tried out to play Squanto in the Thanksgiving pageant.

Meanwhile, Trip and I are kind of sliding back to the way things used to be.

Jacob Gorski's snarky note was right. Without E, we aren't so supercool anymore.

We eat alone in the cafeteria, just like we used to.

We're constantly being called "dweebiac" and "the doofus brothers" again.

Without E's expert coaching, dodgeball in gym class is back to being murderball. Trip and I have the butt bruises to prove it.

Plus, now we have Penelope Pettigrew whining at us every day after school when Maddie signs off and E turns back into E.

"Keep that computerized clodhopper home tomorrow!" she tells me. "He stinks worse than ever. He quit baking toaster tarts and makes pizza rolls now. The ones that smell like they're stuffed with mush-rooms and moldy socks!"

So, like I said, I'm glad Maddie's having such a good time at school.

But, lately, I sort of wish I didn't have to go there with her.

CHAPTER 9

But, of course, I keep going to school.

For one thing, I think it's the law in Indiana. As a kid, you either have to go to school or plant popcorn.

CAN'T LET THE CROPS SIT IN THE SUN TOO LONG ON A HOT DAY. THE KERNELS WILL START A-POPPIN'. NOW GO HOSE DOWN THEM CORN STALKS WITH MOVIE-THEATER BUTTER.

But, mostly, I go to school for Maddie.

After all she's been through on account of her disease—all the trips to the doctor, all the emergency-room visits in the middle of the night, not to mention the in-home IV treatments, plus just the plain loneliness of being the "girl in the bubble" sealed up tight in our sanitized house—it's about time she had some fun and a chance to live a semi-normal life with the help of her amazing blue-eyed robot.

In case I haven't told you yet, let me just say that Maddie Hayes-Rodriguez is the best little sister anybody could ever have. And even though she's younger than me, she seems way wiser. She's always telling me not to worry so much, because "worrying is a waste of imagination." She's also been helping me deal with my fear (make that *terror*) of heights. Last week, with Maddie's help, I stood on the fourth rung of a ladder for five whole minutes.

In the old days (like, three weeks ago), Maddie and I would hang out in her room after dinner, and I'd tell her all about my day at school. Now, when we're done eating, she's kind of busy with her own homework, and then she needs to gab and instant message with

HI, JENNY. DID YOU HEAR WHAT HAPPENED IN THE CAFETERIA TODAY?
HI, SUE. DID I MENTION HOW MUCH I LIKE THE BLINKING LIGHTS IN YOUR SHOES?
HI, LATOYA. CAN YOU TEACH ME HOW TO DO MY HAIR LIKE YOU DO YOURS?

all her new third-grade friends. So we don't hang out like we used to.

But, like I said, it's all good.

Mostly.

Anyway, another Monday rolls around. It's a brand-new week at school. A crisp, clear autumn day. Halloween's just around the corner. Things have got to get better, right?

Wrong.

Turns out there's a new kid in Mrs. Kunkel's class. A guy named Eddie Ingalls. He and his family just moved to South Bend because his father, Professor Ignatius "Iggy" Ingalls, landed a big job at a local college called Indiana Robotics and Automaton Tech (IRAT).

And Eddie didn't come to school alone.

Eddie Ingalls's father sent him to Creekside with a robot.

That's right. Our elementary school now has *two* robots zooming around its halls. The new bot is a six-foot-tall, hulking superhero-looking automaton named SS-10K. He kind of reminds me of the Stormtroopers in the *Star Wars* movies.

"We saw that girl on TV, the one who has a robot going to school for her," Eddie explains to everybody in Mrs. Kunkel's class when he introduces himself. "So I brought one, too. This is the Substitute Student Ten Thousand—SS-10K for short. My father designed him for my brother, Freddy. He's my twin, but Freddy had an accident and can't go to school anymore, so SS-10K goes for him. Say hello to everybody, Freddy."

"Greetings, children!" says the colossal Stormtrooper. He sounds like a G.I. Joe.

I, of course, feel sorry for Freddy. He sounds like he's in the same jam as Maddie.

I'm also a little jealous of Eddie.

He has an awesome robot and I don't.

CHAPTER 10

When it's time for recess, Trip and I hurry out the door, chasing after Eddie Ingalls and his shiny new robot just like everybody else in Mrs. Kunkel's class.

"That SS-10K has to be the most amazing robotic marvel ever invented!" declares Jacob Gorski. "He's way better than that hunk of junk E."

Then he bops his forehead like he just had a major brainstorm.

"Hey, you guys! I just had an awesome idea. One day after school, the Robotics Club should sponsor a Rock'em Sock'em Robots boxing match! It'll be a life-sized version of that game by Mattel. SS-10K and E can go glove-to-glove until one of them knocks the other's block off."

"Fantabulous idea," gushes Penelope Pettigrew. "It could be a fund-raiser. All the money would go to medical charities—ones that E will definitely need after SS-10K knocks his head off his shoulders!"

After school, I tell Trip that I want to bike home with E alone.

"Sure," says Trip. "I understand. You guys need to talk over strategy and tactics for the Rock'em Sock'em Robots boxing match."

"Trip, are you crazy? No way am I letting E step into a ring to go up against a major muscle machine like that. E was built to go to school for Maddie, not to get in fights."

"You're right. He'd get creamed. See you tomorrow."

Trip takes off.

On our ride home, when Maddie's no longer the one controlling E, I tell him about Jacob Gorski's wacky idea.

"An interesting notion," says E. "I am not averse to boxing a few rounds, if it's for charity."

"But you saw that thing. SS-10K is enormous."

"True. But this boxing game would be all in good fun."

"I don't know. The new robot doesn't strike me as a 'fun' guy."

E places a gentle hand on my shoulder. "As Maddie might say, don't worry so much, Sammy. Robots are your friends. We're only here to help. It's why we were created. To be helpful."

Maybe.

But I can't help thinking that robots can be hurtful, too.

Especially if they punch you in your jaw.

CHAPTER 11

I guess you could say I'm conflicted.

Or confused. Maybe both.

On the one hand, I think it's fantastic that Eddie Ingalls's twin brother is able to go to school thanks to a robot, just like Maddie.

On the other hand, I think I'm sort of jealous. Eddie's robot is bigger and stronger than mine. And my robot isn't even mine anymore. During the school day, he belongs to Maddie.

Maybe I should ask Mom to give E more muscles. Less of a smile. More of a sneer.

And instead of a goofy baseball cap, maybe E could wear a mask and a cape, like a superhero or something. It doesn't matter that E is supposed to be Maddie during school days. Lots of girls are super-heroes, too.

I decide to discuss my redesign idea with Mom.

MEET THE NEW AND IMPROVED E. I'VE BEEN SUPERSIZED.

I head to her workshop next door to the house because, even though it's way after din-ner, she's still over there working.

"Sorry, hon," she says. "I'm really busy. Mr. Riley and some of the other major Notre Dame donors want to license the research I did to create Egghead to a company out in California that will mass-produce 'stand-in-bots' for home-bound people all over the country. I have to finish this paperwork, fast. Apparently we have some major competition out there."

"You do. A new kid in my class brought a robot to school that does exactly the same stuff for his sick brother that E does for Maddie."

"Dr. Ignatius Ingalls's son?"

"Yep. Do you know him?"

"Oh, yes. Dr. Ingalls and I went to the same high school."

"Really?"

"Yep. Back then, a lot of girls called him Icky."

"How come?"

Mom grinned. "It's not important, Sammy. I'd heard that Dr. Ingalls was moving here to head up IRAT. I did not, however, know he had a prototype helper-bot already online."

"It's called the Substitute Student Ten Thousand. SS-10K for short."

"I guess that means I need to work faster. And harder. Was there something you needed to talk about, Sammy?"

"No. That's okay. I'll just ask Dad."

So I go back inside and find Dad crumpling up sketches at his drawing table.

"This is terrible," I hear him mumble.

Uh-oh. This can't be good. See, my father, Noah Rodriguez, is also Sasha Nee. That's the pen name he uses for this supercool, bestselling graphic novel series he writes and illustrates called *Hot and Sour Ninja Robots*. He usually likes the pictures he draws. Tonight? Not so much.

He sees me kind of lurking near his desk, when he wads up another sketch and adds it to his paper-ball collection all over the floor.

"Sammy!" he says. "Have you heard any kids at school talking about this new graphic novel *Sweet and Spicy Samurai Warriors*?"

I nod because I have.

My dad looks panicked. "Do they like it?"

"I guess," I say with a shrug. "I heard some fifth graders saying they were going to dress up like Sweet and Spicy for Halloween."

When I say that, Dad starts tugging at his hair.

"Gorzzlesnout!" he says, then starts scribbling crazily on his sketchpad. That's usually something the bad guys say in his comic books. And only when they know they're totally trapped, with no way out.

O-kay. Maybe this isn't the best time to have a chat with Dad.

But I have to discuss all this stuff with somebody, or my head might explode off my shoulders even without SS-10K bopping me under my chin.

So I do what I always do when I really need to talk.

I head to Maddie's room.

CHAPTER 12

Most people who visit Maddie's room have to wear sterile hospital masks.

Not me. I guess we have the same germs.

I do, however, always wash my hands real good and squirt 'em with sanitizer from one of the many pumps mounted on the walls all over our house.

I knock on her door.

"Come on in!" Maddie cries out. "We're doing homework! Marvelous, glorious homework! And tomorrow, guess what? We're having a spelling test! Woo-hoo!"

Yep. Maddie really, really, *really* likes going to

school. I guess I would, too, if I couldn't ever really leave my room.

She sees me sort of slouching in the doorway.

"Are you okay, Sammy?" she asks.

"Yeah. Fine."

"You look worried. Again."

"I am."

"Perhaps I can be of assistance," says E. "Has someone asked you to climb to an elevated height?

Logically, we know that things that might trigger a fear of heights—skyscrapers, airplanes, and roller coasters, for instance..."

Ooof. He's making me queasy.

"...are incredibly safe."

"It's not my fear of heights," I say as fast as I can because my face is turning green. "It's that new robot in my class. SS-10K."

"Are you upset because he's so popular?" asks Maddie.

"A little."

"I'm not. Now that E isn't the most famous robot at school, we have more quiet time to study."

"But," I say, "a couple kids want SS-10K to fight E."

Maddie giggles. "That's silly. E's a scholar, not a fighter."

"However," says E, "as I informed Sammy earlier, I am not averse to engaging in a pugilistic competition if it is for a charitable cause. Boxing has been called the 'sport of kings,' although I do not recall ever seeing two kings step into the ring to duke it out."

"I'm also kind of jealous," I admit. "SS-10K is getting all the attention E and I used to get."

"There's room for more than one robot at school, Sammy," says Maddie. "And being voted most popular isn't what this is all about."

"I guess…"

"Hey, maybe you should ask Mom to let you take one of her other robots to school with you."

"But I don't need a robot."

"All humans need robots," says E. "We make everything, including education, a little easier."

"They also attract quite a crowd," adds Maddie.

For the first time all day, I smile.

Maybe if I have my own robot, I'll be super popular again.

I kind of like this idea. Maybe I need a helper-bot, too.

One to help me be cool again.

CHAPTER 13

I was going to ask Mom to get permission from school. Honest. I was.

But the next morning is crazy busy.

The Breakfastinator is on the fritz, spewing globby oatmeal with blueberries all over Maddie's not-so-clean-anymore room.

Hayseed, our gardener-bot, is trying to fix it. With a rake.

DING!

DING!

DING!

READY

SPLAT!

STAND BACK.
THIS THING IS A FEW PEAS
SHY OF A CASSEROLE.

DO YOU KNOW HOW HARD
IT IS TO GET BLUEBERRY
STAINS OUT OF CURTAINS?

Maddie isn't really interested in eating her flying breakfast. She's busy cramming for her spelling test.

"F-R-I, E-N-D, because I am a friend to the end."

Downstairs, in his home office, Dad is on the phone. I think he just got some bad news from his

publisher.

Meanwhile, next door in her workshop, Mom is

busy tinkering with E's video inputs.

"The monitor in Maddie's control pod has been flickering," she says when I poke my head in to ask her about taking one of the other robots to school with me. "I need to reset the system management controller. You go on to school, Sammy. E will be running a little late."

"Okay, but I need to ask you something—"

"Ask your father, okay, hon? I'm kind of busy."

She jabs a circuit board inside the back of E's head with a smoldering solder iron.

Guess E's sort of out of it this morning, too.

So I dash back to our house, where Dad is tugging at his hair and chewing on a pencil like he's a beaver taking a snack break. There are flecks of yellow paint chips all over his teeth.

"Dad? Is it okay with you if—"

"Yes, fine, whatever," he answers before I even ask my question, because he's not really paying attention. "I can't believe they're pulling the plug. No more *Hot and Sour Ninja Robots*? One minute you're a hero, the next you're a zero...."

I sort of tiptoe out of the room and let him mumble to himself some more.

Then I head out to the backyard to switch on Blitzen, the linebacker-slash-lawn-mower-bot.

Quick background on Blitzen: Every year at Notre Dame, my mom's College of Engineering hosts this National Robotics Week Blue-Gold robot football game—aka the Robot Bowl—featuring the Fighting iBots (instead of the Fighting Irish, which is what ND calls their

humanoid football team). Blitzen was the star of the game last year.

Blitzen retired from robot football so he could cut our grass, but he still has a lot of the game etched into his microchips.

I can't wait to show him off at school.

Maybe he'll even dive-tackle SS-10K!

CHAPTER 14

Blitzen is awesome!" says Trip as he locks up his bike on the rack in front of school.

We both hang there for a minute to watch Blitzen buzz around in a nearby patch of grass, attacking dandelions.

"Yellow, fifty-two!" Blitzen barks like a quarterback at the line of scrimmage. "Yellow, fifty-two! Omaha. Hut-hut-hut." Then he rumbles off to gobble up more grass, weeds, and even a few rocks, which clunk around under his cutting deck.

"Wow," says Trip. "He'll eat anything. So instead of E doing it, maybe Blitzen could show everybody how cool I am by gobbling down a peanut-butter-and-banana sandwich."

"Maybe," I say. "We'll see how hungry he is at lunchtime. Come on, we need to hurry inside. Mom might be driving E to school today."

"So? She knows you brought Blitzen with you this morning. Right?"

"Um, not exactly."

"Hoo-boy."

When we get to our classroom and Blitzen, motor humming, parks next to my desk, Mrs. Kunkel asks the question I really should've figured out an answer for by now.

"Sammy? Why did you bring one of your mother's other robots to school today?"

"That thing's electrical motor is creating electromagnetic static for SS-10K," complains Eddie Ingalls. "My poor, sick brother, Freddy, can't see the board clearly with all the interference." He touches a high-tech Bluetooth device he has jammed into his right ear. "Now you've done it, Sammy Hayes-Rodriguez. You and your stupid lawn-mowing linebacker have made Freddy cry. In my ear."

"Samuel?" says Mrs. Kunkel.

Uh-oh. When anybody uses my full name like that, I know I'm in trouble.

"Yes, ma'am?"

"I think it might be best if your robot waited out in the hall. We can discuss this further at recess."

"Okay." I look down at Blitzen. He has voice-recognition software, so I can just tell him what to do. "Hit the hall. On three. Hut-hut-hut."

"Break!" Blitzen shouts, twirls around, and rolls toward the door.

Which he bumps into.

Repeatedly.

In that Fighting iBot football game, Blitzen was mostly a tackler. He just sort of plowed into stuff. He didn't really need hands to catch or throw a ball. Or to open doors.

I leap out of my seat, run to the door, and open it.

"Wait out here," I say.

"You got it, Coach."

And I'm sure Blitzen would've done what I told him to do.

Except the linoleum in the hallways of Creekside Elementary is a sparkling emerald green.

The color of grass. On a football field.

And since it stretches out in a straight line for maybe fifty yards, I guess it sort of *looks* like a football field, too, a very skinny one.

So Blitzen's task-recognition software naturally alerts him that it's time to mow the tile and score a touchdown.

I guess it's a good thing SS-10K is in Mrs. Kunkel's classroom.

When we all hear the commotion out in the corridor, Dr. Ingalls's robot immediately stands up and asks the teacher for a hall pass.

"I do not wish to alarm you or your students," he says in a deep, steady voice. "But I sense mayhem and mischief nearby. Intruder alert! Intruder alert! Must have hall pass!"

I've never seen Mrs. Kunkel scribble faster.

Hall pass in hand, SS-10K races out the door, tackles Blitzen, and yanks out his batteries.

"Mission accomplished," he reports as he comes back into the room, clutching a dangling Blitzen by his power cables.

"Thank you, SS-10K," says Mrs. Kunkel. Then she starts scribbling on her yellow hall-pass pad again. When she fills in all the blanks, she rips it out and hands it to me.

So I could go to the principal's office.

With my broken bot, Blitzen.

CHAPTER 15

Blitzen and I have to wait on the "uh-oh" chair outside Mrs. Reyes's office.

Everybody calls it the "uh-oh" chair because if you're sitting on it, you probably, *uh-oh*, did something seriously wrong.

I'VE BEEN BENCHED.

PRINCIPAL

Mom shows up and, basically, doesn't say anything. She just shakes her head, clucks her tongue, and says, "Samuel, Samuel, Samuel."

Yep. I'm in trouble. Big-time.

When we're called into Mrs. Reyes's office to hear my punishment, the grown-ups decide that it might be best "for everybody" if I went home and spent the day thinking about the consequences of my actions.

"Somebody could've been hurt, Sammy," says Mrs. Reyes. "At Creekside Elementary, we like to keep our lawn mowers outside. On the lawn."

The ride home is kind of quiet.

Until Mom sighs and says, "Do you need a babysitter-bot, Sammy? Because if you do, I could build you one."

"No. I don't need a babysitter. Robotic or human."

"So what's going on here?"

"Nothing."

Yep. I give her the classic kid answer (because it's all I can come up with on such short notice).

"Are you jealous that E is going to school for Maddie now?"

"No," I say. "I think that's great. I think what you did for Maddie is amazing."

That makes her smile some—a nearly impossible feat, by the way, thirty minutes after you've been sent home by the principal for wreaking havoc in the hallways with an out-of-control piece of robotic gardening equipment.

So I keep going, piling on the compliments.

"What you did is absolutely phenomenal. After all these years, Maddie can finally go to a real school without, you know, really going to school."

"Well, if you change your mind about the babysitter, I could always reconfigure that antique nannybot who used to change your diapers...."

"Mom, for the last time, I don't need a babysitter."

I think a little longer.

"But a bodyguard-bot might be nice."

Mom punctures my thought balloon fast.

"Sammy?"

STAND BACK. MAKE WAY. DO NOT MAKE ME TEACH YOU A LESSON, EVEN THOUGH, TECHNICALLY, WE ARE AT SCHOOL.

"Yeah?"

"Not gonna happen."

"Yeah. Didn't think so."

But, hey, a kid can dream, can't he?

CHAPTER 16

The next morning, I start thinking that maybe Mom is the one who needs a bodyguard, to protect her from Professor Ignatius "Iggy" Ingalls over at IRAT, which, come to think of it, sounds like a rodent version of iTunes.

Dad, who is still bummed out about losing his book contract (his hair is sticking straight up, electrocution-style, from all the tugging he's been doing on it lately), is dressed in pajamas and slurping down a bowl of cereal while watching the morning news.

Dr. Ingalls is being interviewed. SS-10K, arms folded across his chest, is sitting right beside him. The hulking robot's helmet visor is glowing red, like he's mad about something.

Dr. Ingalls doesn't look very happy, either.

"I'm with Professor 'Iggy' Ingalls," chirps the cheery morning-show reporter, "from Indiana Robotics and Automaton Tech. So, who's this big, handsome guy you brought with you?"

"That," says Dr. Ingalls, "is the Substitute Student Ten Thousand. I designed, engineered, and built him to go to school for my unfortunate son, Freddy, who was in a terrible, horrible, tragic accident."

"Say, is your SS-10K anything like that robot E

from Notre Dame? The one who, as our viewers saw just last week, is going to school for the inventor's homebound daughter?"

Dr. Ingalls gives the reporter a polite titter. "Hardly. I, of course, applaud Dr. Elizabeth Hayes and her colleagues at the University of Notre Dame for their early, pioneering efforts in the field of substitute student robotics. Her work, although primitive and somewhat childish, paved the way for technological leaps such as SS-10K."

"Did he just call Mom primitive?" I ask.

Dad nods. "And somewhat childish."

"I don't like Professor Ingalls."

Mom steps into the breakfast nook. "Join the club," she says, sipping coffee that isn't steaming as much as she is. "Now you know why, back in high school, we all called him Icky."

"Nothing personal," says Professor Ingalls (which means he's probably about to say something very nasty), "but Dr. Hayes's robots are nothing more than gadgets, gewgaws, and gizmos. Toys you play with on Christmas morning and toss out by New Year's Day. They might also be dangerous. Apparently, there was an unfortunate incident yesterday at the school involving one of Dr. Hayes's rampaging robots. Luckily, my SS-10K was able to quickly restore order."

Oops.

I didn't realize that somebody Instagrammed that.

"On the other hand," Dr. Ingalls continues, "SS-10K is a safe, sophisticated, and self-sufficient servant for all of humanity!"

"Yes," says the robot. "I am here to serve humans."

Yikes.

When SS-10K says it, he sounds like McDonald's talking about serving hamburgers.

CHAPTER 17

Things are pretty grim around the robot house.

Dad says he may "never draw again."

And Mom—along with everything she's been work-ing on since before I was born—has been totally burned on TV because of me.

As we're biking with Trip to school, E can see that I'm feeling kind of blue.

"Why so glum, chum?" he chirps.

"Dad's not doing so well. They canceled his graphic novel series."

"Everybody's reading that new comic book," says Trip. "The one about the two samurai guys. Itchy and Scratchy."

I correct him. "Sweet and Spicy."

"Not to worry," says E. "Mr. Noah Rodriguez is an extremely talented artist. He will generate a new creative idea. Soon. You'll see. Something even better."

"How can you be so sure?" I ask.

"Because I find positive energy to be much more useful than the negative variety."

The three of us bike down the road.

"Well, what about that new guy, Dr. Ingalls from IRAT?" I ask. "He was making fun of Mom on TV. Said her robots are nothing but gewgaws, gizmos, and gadgets."

"That means you're like an electric can opener or something," adds Trip.

"Sticks and stones may break my bones, but names will never hurt me. Unless, of course, the stones being hurled also have names. For instance, the gemstones malachite, melanite, moldavite..."

"Are you and Maddie studying geology in Ms. Tracey's class?" I ask.

"Yes. How did you know?"

I shrug. "Lucky guess."

We park our bikes and hurry into school.

Penelope Pettigrew is waiting for us. Actually, she's kind of blocking the whole hallway.

"Kindly step aside and let us pass, Miss Pettigrew," says E, still trying to stay positive.

I'm not as good at that as he is. "Move out of the way, Penelope. And quit saying mean junk about my sister."

"Yeah." That's Trip. "What Sammy and E said."

But Penelope doesn't budge. "You know, Maddie, you really need to do something about your smile. Maybe you could find a dentist to fill that gap between your teeth. You could lose a chipmunk in that thing."

"Actually," says E, extremely calmly, "I am not

currently being operated by Maddie, who, trust me, has the sweetest smile in the world. It could, as they say, light up a room. I apologize, however, if you find my own dental hardware in any way offensive."

I hear a *ZHUSH-WHIRR-ZHUSH* behind us.

In marches Eddie Ingalls and SS-10K. The heroic bot bumps into E's back like one of those Roomba vacuum cleaners that scoot around the carpet until they smack into a wall.

E turns around and looks up at the hulking robot.

KINDLY STEP ASIDE. OCCUPANCY OF THIS SPACE BY MORE THAN ONE ROBOT AT THE SAME TIME IS UNSAFE.

SS-10K

"Who are you?" drones SS-10K. "Please identify yourself."

"I am E. Short for Egghead."

"Yeah," says Penelope. "Because you smell like a rotten egg."

"Actually," I say, "my mom calls E Egghead because he's superintelligent."

"Well, if he's so smart," says snarky Penelope, "what's he doing hanging out with you?"

"Ooh," says Eddie Ingalls. "Score."

He does that stupid thing where he licks his finger and pretends to mark a 1 with it on some kind of invisible scoreboard.

I hate when people do that.

"I understand that you and I share similar primary functions," E says very politely. I guess this is how robots make small talk with each other.

"Affirmative," says SS-10K. "And, currently, you are prohibiting me from fulfilling my mission. Kindly step to one side."

SS-10K puts a hand on E's shoulder like he might shove E out of the way.

"Move it," says Eddie. "Our robot needs to go to school for my brother, Teddy."

E nods and moonwalks out of the way.

"Wait a second," I say. "I thought your twin brother's name was Freddy, not Teddy."

"Freddy is what everybody calls him. But, uh, his full name is Theodore Frederick Ingalls. Or *Teddy Freddy*." He turns to Penelope. "You need to move out of our way, too. Now."

"Sure thing." She skips down the hall, giggling.

"See you in class, Sammy," says Eddie as he and SS-10K proceed down the hall. "You, too, what's-your-name."

"I'm Trip. Well, that's what Sammy calls me. My real name is..."

Eddie and his robot aren't listening. They keep forging ahead.

"I'll tell you later," says Trip.

Even though SS-10K isn't exactly friendly to E, my bro-bot stays sunny-side up.

"And might I congratulate you, SS-10K, for executing your mission so well here at Creekside Elementary School?"

SS-10K doesn't look back. He just says, "We are here to serve humans."

With a side of fries, I want to say, because, once again, I'm thinking about McDonald's.

Then the new robot says, "Study hard, Eggbert."

And E doesn't correct him.

I guess that should've been my first hint that something was wrong.

Really, really wrong.

CHAPTER 18

About an hour later, a voice comes over the intercom in Mrs. Kunkel's room.

SAMMY HAYES-RODRIGUEZ, PLEASE REPORT TO MS. TRACEY'S THIRD-GRADE CLASSROOM.

"Guess they're sending you back where you belong," cracks Jacob Gorski, my geeky new bully. "Third grade!"

Of course he says it so softly that Mrs. Kunkel, who's busy at the Smart Board, can't hear him.

"You'd better go, Sammy," says Mrs. Kunkel. "Maddie must need something."

"Yes, ma'am."

I hurry down the hall.

When I step into Ms. Tracey's room, it's bedlam.

"Make him stop doing that!" screeches Penelope Pettigrew.

E is up at the front of the classroom, dancing some kind of crazy jig.

Ms. Tracey has her arms spread out like a soccer goalie, protecting the little kids in their seats from the big, jangling robot who's flapping his arms and legs like a marionette with its strings tangled up in a ceiling fan.

Maddie's voice peeps out of E's mouth. "Something's wrong, Sammy. E isn't doing what I tell him to do."

"He's demented!" shouts Penelope.

"Demented," says E. "D-E, M-E, that's me. N-T, E-D, E-I-E-I-O!"

Penelope is defending herself by flinging paper clips at E. She has, like, a whole pencil bag full of the things. "He's dangerous! Make him stop!" Her paper clips bonk off E's metal head and bounce to the floor.

"We were taking our spelling test," says Ms. Tracey over her shoulder. "Then E started dancing."

"My word was *samba*, Sammy," says E, shaking his clamper-claws and making *SHIKKA-SHIKKA* maraca sounds.

"Maddie?" I cry out.

"Yes, Sammy?"

"Switch E to internal control mode."

E's blazing blue LED eyeballs flicker a little. That means Maddie just passed off control to the bot.

"E?" I say, moving slowly up an aisle between desks. "It's me. Sammy."

"My brother? Samuel Hayes-Rodriguez? R-O-D-R..."

"Yes, E. It's me. You need to settle down."

E's limbs go all loose, and he collapses to the floor. "I have settled down."

"Good. You have to obey Ms. Tracey's rules, too."

"I have memorized Ms. Tracey's rules for punctuation. A statement is followed by a period. A period of rain is good for a garden. A garden is good for growing gophers."

I can't believe it. E is having a major microchip meltdown. He keeps rattling off all sorts of random third-grade gobbledygook.

"Make him stop!" cries Penelope Pettigrew. "Please, MAKE HIM STOP!" Then she puts her arm to her forehead and swoons backward in her seat. She's kind of dramatic that way.

"Sammy?" says Ms. Tracey. "You need to pull E's plug."

She's right. I have no choice.

"Sorry, bro," I say as I reach around E's back and flip his emergency shutdown switch.

There's a quick *WHIRR-CLICK* and a *SNIZZLE-FLICK*. E's head droops. His chin clunks into his chest. The light is gone from his eyes.

When he's nothing but a limp heap of aluminum, the school janitor helps me haul E down to the principal's office.

I get to sit on the "uh-oh" chair (again) while we wait for Mom to come pick us up (again).

The school secretary clucks her tongue at us.

"What a shame," she says. "Too bad E can't be more like SS-10K. What a nice boy that robot is. Such a gentleman."

"Yes, ma'am" is all I can say.

But I tap the silent E on his knee because I don't really mean it.

CHAPTER 19

"I don't know what's wrong with E," says Mom after we haul him home to her workshop.

I've never seen her so down in the dumps.

WHY DO MY ROBOTS KEEP ACTING UP IN SCHOOL? DO THEY NEED TO EAT A BETTER BREAKFAST BEFORE THEY LEAVE HOME?

First Dr. Ingalls insults her on TV. Then E goes bananas at school. What's next? The Breakfastinator starts making lunch?

"I must be losing my touch," Mom says with a very heavy sigh.

"No, you're not," I say, hoping to buck her up with my positive energy, the kind E always tries to use. "It's probably something ridiculously simple. You'll figure it out."

She shakes her head. "I'm not so sure, Sammy. Maybe this whole 'substitute student' project wasn't a wise use of my time or the engineering school's resources."

"What? Sending Maddie, and kids just like her, to school—*real* school—when they can't go themselves? That wasn't a good thing for you guys to try to do? What could Notre Dame be working on that's more important than that? A robotic toaster that can handle bagels without them ever getting stuck?"

"That's a pretty good idea...."

"Mom? I was kidding."

"I know. Run to the kitchen. Fix yourself a sandwich or a bowl of soup." She rolls up her sleeves. Grabs a tiny screwdriver from her toolbox. "I won't be cooking dinner tonight."

Good. She's not giving up.

Not just yet, anyway.

Later, Maddie and I are hanging out in her room, pretending to be doing our homework. Mostly, we're thinking about E. And Mom.

And Maddie being stuck in her room forever, with no eyes or ears out in the real world.

Yes, for maybe the first time ever, even Maddie is worried.

When all their chores are done, some of the robots roll into Maddie's room to wait and worry with us.

All of a sudden, E strides into the room looking as good as new!

"Are you okay?" asks Maddie.

"Never better. Dr. Elizabeth Hayes, the finest robotics engineer in all the land, adjusted my voltage regulator, my photoelectric sensors, and my inverting encoder. She also removed a metal object that was crossing circuits in my motherboard. I feel fantastic. Fit as a fiddle, bright as a button, fresh as a daisy, and good as new."

"We've been studying similes in Ms. Tracey's class," explains Maddie.

"If you don't mind my asking, old bean," says Geoffrey, the butler-bot, "why were you madder than a monkey on a motor scooter this morning?"

"My malfunction," says E, "was caused, we think, by a paper clip flicked into my ear canal. We believe its metal made contact with my internal wiring, thereby shorting out my functionality grid."

"Penelope Pettigrew!" I say. "I saw her flinging paper clips at your head."

"We have no evidence that Miss Pettigrew was the perpetrator," says E. "I am simply grateful to once again be fully functional. I hope to be heading back to school first thing tomorrow morning."

"Yippee!" says Maddie.

Yes, she's that excited.

"Wait a second," I say. "What if whoever did this tries to chuck some other tiny chunk of metal into your head holes? A staple, maybe. Or a bobby pin."

"Not to worry, Sammy. Mom just installed a thin but impenetrable plastic mesh over my ear openings. My hearing will not be impaired, just the ability of foreign objects to enter my cranial cavity."

"Um, is your cranial cavity the same thing as your head?"

"Indeed so, Sammy."

"So you'll be fine going back to school for Maddie?"

E nods. Maddie beams.

"All the necessary attitude adjustments have been made," says E. "Mom has certified me as good to go. What happened at school today won't happen again."

If the school lets E come back, I think.

And that's a big *if*.

CHAPTER 20

The next morning, in the principal's office, Mom makes an impassioned plea to Mrs. Reyes for E to be allowed back in the third-grade classroom.

Dad and I are there to cheer her and E on.

"This isn't just about my daughter," Mom tells Mrs. Reyes. "If we can prove that robots like E can safely function in a schoolroom setting..."

"Like SS-10K is doing, you mean," says Mrs. Reyes.

O-kay. That made Mom wince a little. But she keeps plugging.

"I'm glad Dr. Ingalls and his team at IRAT are also exploring the field of robotic stand-ins for home-bound students," she says. "The more colleges and technical schools working on this idea, the better."

"But Lizzie had the idea first," says Dad, who came along for the meeting because, as he put it, "I didn't have anything else to do today."

Yes, he's been kind of pouty (and unshaven) ever since his publisher canceled his book contract.

"E's problems are solved," Mom assures Principal Reyes. "He can function just as safely and maybe even more effectively than the Substitute Student Ten Thousand."

"As long as nobody pokes him in the ear with a paper clip," says Dad.

Mom shoots him a look. It's the same look I get when I'm goofing around in church.

Dad holds up both hands like he surrenders. I

notice that his hands aren't stained with ink like they usually are.

Wow. He really is throwing in the towel.

"Somebody jabbed E with a paper clip?" asks Principal Reyes.

Mom nods. "I found a bent piece of thin metal lodged inside E's cranial cavity."

"That's his head," I say, just to be helpful.

"Once the foreign object was removed, I gave E's operating system a total reboot. Long story short, he is ready to go back to work. For Maddie."

"And for all humanity," adds E. "Rest assured, Principal Reyes, my problems have been solved so that Maddie might solve more math problems. She particularly enjoys word problems, especially the ones about two trains leaving different cities at different times."

"You make a strong case," says Mrs. Reyes. "But I have to be honest, guys. I'm still not sure. What's that old saying? 'Science never solves a problem without creating ten more.'"

"A quote by George Bernard Shaw," says E, probably just to show Mrs. Reyes that he's operating on all cylinders. "Mr. Shaw, however, was an Irish playwright, not a scientist."

Oh yeah. E's supersmart when he's not nutty.

"Point taken," says Mrs. Reyes. "But…"

E's eyeballs flicker.

"Please, Mrs. Reyes?"

It's Maddie. Speaking through E.

WHEN I'M AT SCHOOL, I'M A PART OF SOMETHING MUCH BIGGER THAN ME. SCHOOL IS HELPING ME BECOME MORE OF A CITIZEN AND LESS OF A CHILD. EDUCATION ISN'T JUST PREPARATION FOR LIFE; EDUCATION IS LIFE ITSELF! PLEASE, MRS. REYES. LET ME KEEP ON LEARNING AND LIVING!

"We promise to be good," she says. "Going to school means so much to me."

Her voice is choked with emotion.

E's big, blue eyeballs are getting kind of watery, too.

There isn't a dry eye in the principal's office.

E is given one more chance.

If you ask me, Mom did an absolutely awesome job fixing E.

School goes great. E is better than good. In fact, he's fantastic.

From what Maddie tells me when I check back in with her at lunchtime, things couldn't be going better.

"Everything's wonderful," she tells me.

There are no loudspeaker announcements calling me down to the third-grade classroom.

No snide comments from Creekside Robotics Club president Jacob Gorski.

Even Eddie Ingalls leaves me alone.

As soon as school is done for the day, Maddie switches E to internal control mode so he can be my bro-bot on the bike ride home.

"See you guys later," Maddie says before signing off. "And, Sammy?"

"Yeah?"

"I *LOOOOOOOVE* going to school! Maddie out."

E's eyeballs do their blue flicker dance.

"Good to be back on the job matriculating," he says.

"Good to have you here," I say.

SS-10K is also proud to see E back on the job, doing his duty as Maddie's substitute student. He strides across the parking lot with a hearty, arm-chugging *ZHURR, ZHURR, ZHURR* as E and I mount our bikes.

The big bot even shakes E's hand. "You have made me proud to be a substitute student like you, only incredibly better. Given your severely limited operating system and your inferior circuitry, you did quite well this day. Keep up the good work, Eggbeater. Remember: We are here to serve humans. Now, if you will excuse me, Freddy and I have homework to do."

E and I watch SS-10K march away—arms swinging, knees pumping.

"I don't like that bot," I say. "He's a big, fat phony."

"Of course he is, Sammy. He is a robot. By definition, his intelligence is artificial and, therefore, not real, or, as you call it, phony."

"Fine. But, for whatever reason, the big bucket of bolts just makes me angry."

"If I might be permitted to quote Buddha..."

"Sure. Go ahead. Knock yourself out."

"'Holding on to anger is like grasping a hot coal with the intent of throwing it at someone else; you are the one who gets burned.'"

"Maybe. But Buddha never had to go to school with Penelope Pettigrew, Eddie Ingalls, or SS-10K."

CHAPTER 22

The next morning, our house is buzzing along like usual.

As Maddie might say, it's another "grand and glorious" school day.

Downstairs, Dingaling, the doorbell-bot out on our front porch, starts swinging his hand bell.

"Someone's at the door," I say, slurping down my cereal.

"I wonder who it is." Maddie slurps back. "It's awfully early."

Dingaling rings again. Louder. He's very annoying that way.

"Sammy?" Dad hollers up the stairs, sounding kind of crabby. "Can you please go see who the heck that is? I'm trying to think up a new idea for a graphic novel, and all I can come up with right now is a story about a church bell battling the Liberty Bell and they both get headaches!"

"No problem, Dad," I shout, quickly spooning one more clump of cereal into my mouth.

E places a firm hand on my shoulder. "Finish your breakfast, Sammy. It's the most important meal of the day. Students who skip breakfast do not do as well at school as those who eat it. I will go deal with whoever is at the door."

"Thanks," I say, my mouth full of soggy, mushy food.

E troops downstairs. When Maddie and I are finally done slurping and "nom, nom, nomming," she says, "I'm so glad I still get to go to school."

"Me too."

"The whole third grade is going to start working on science project ideas today!"

"Cool."

"I might show how a compass works with chopsticks, a glass, a magnet, some string, tape, and graph paper."

"I'd be happy to help you with that," says E as he motors back into Maddie's bedroom.

He's covered with word magnets. Those tiny ones that come in a kit so you can make refrigerator poetry.

I check out E's butt.

The magnetic phrase back there is "I mustache you to kick me."

"Um, E?" I ask. "Who was at the door?"

"Penelope Pettigrew, the girl who sits behind me in Ms. Tracey's class. She said she wanted Maddie, that is, me, to look 'prettier' today and kindly volunteered to decorate my torso with what she called temporary word tattoos."

I start peeling the rubbery magnets off E's metallic skin.

"She's making fun of you," I say.

"And me," adds Maddie.

"Really?" says E, who, I sometimes forget, still needs help being an eight-year-old kid. "But I think these magnetic decorations might make us more socially acceptable at school."

"No," I say. "They'll only make people laugh at you."

"Why would Penelope want people laughing at me?" asks E innocently.

"Because she is studying to be a Mean Girl by the time she gets to middle school," says Maddie.

"I apologize," says E, dropping his head. "I did not fully understand her motives."

"Wait here," I say, because E looks so sad.

I dash down the hall to pull something off a metal cabinet I have in my bedroom. I bring it back to E and slap it on his shoulder.

"Now, that's a temporary tattoo you can wear with pride!"

It's my Notre Dame Fighting Irish magnet.

"I am honored to wear this magnet, Sammy," E says proudly. "I went to the University of Notre Dame. I remember meeting a very attractive vending machine. Her GPS coordinates will forever remain in my memory."

It's true. E went to ND once with Mom. It was, basically, a college-level show-and-tell session.

The alarm in my smartphone starts chirping. It's eight AM. School starts in twenty minutes.

"We'd better go," I say, grabbing my backpack.

"And, E?" says Maddie.

"Yes?"

"Try to avoid Penelope Pettigrew today."

E actually grins. "Of course. I will make that my secondary primary objective."

CHAPTER 23

Trip meets us at the corner, and the three of us bike off to school.

It's a perfect fall morning.

I tell Trip how Penelope Pettigrew dropped by the house to plaster E with magnetic graffiti.

"Why is that girl so nasty?" he asks as we pedal down the block.

"I think she's kind of jealous," I say. "She might've been the star of Ms. Tracey's class until Maddie and E showed up."

"Well, you need to keep far away from her," Trip tells E. "Don't let her sit too close. If you want, I can loan you an old peanut-butter-and-banana sandwich that I forgot I had in the bottom of my lunch bag. It's kind of moldy. Rotten banana stench is a smell that usually scares people away."

"Thank you, Trip," says E. "B-b-but I don't think I w-w-want to smell b-b-bad."

"Are you okay?" I ask.

"Fine and dandy, like cotton candy. Look good, feel better. I'm super-duper A-OK."

E sounds like a rolling computer glitch. I'm wondering if all those magnets Penelope slapped on his skin warped something inside his microchips, the same way magnets can damage cell phones.

"You sure you don't want a sandwich, E?" says Trip. "If you unwrap it and put it on your desk, I'll bet Penelope Pettigrew won't want to sit in the row right behind you anymore..."

All of a sudden, E starts singing.

"Row, row, row your boat, gently down the stream..."

He sounds like a bad episode of *Sesame Street*.

"E?" I say. "We need to take you home. Right now. Penelope Pettigrew magnetically scrambled your brain!"

PENELOPE PETTIGREW PICKED A PECK OF PICKLED PEPPERS AND POKED A POKER AT THE PIPER SO PETER PICKED PEAS FOR THE POOR PINK PIG.

"I'm serious, E. If you goof up at school again…"

"Hasta la vista, Señor Rodriguez!"

E turbo-pumps his bicycle and blasts off.

We're near the same pet store in the same strip mall we pass every morning, but this morning, we don't actually *pass* it. E veers off course and zips into the parking lot.

He hops off his bike and tears into the shop.

"Jailbreak!" he screams.

With the help of the shopkeeper, Trip and I are able to corral most of the critters and put them back in their cages.

But while we were doing that, E slipped out of the pet shop.

Trip and I race outside.

"How do you like your eggs, Sammy?"

I whip around.

It's E.

He comes out of the convenience store next door to the pet shop with maybe three dozen eggs, some plastic-wrapped snacks tucked under his arm, and a sixteen-pack of toilet paper.

"How about scrambled?" shouts E. "Just like my brain!"

He holds up an egg, aims right for us...and then fires!

CHAPTER 24

E actually starts egging Trip and me!

"This is the real reason they call me Egghead!"

While he's pelting us, E also starts laughing like a mechatronic maniac.

Trip and I duck and cover while shouting at E to stop. We have egg yolks splattered all over our school clothes and gooey egg whites dripping from our hair.

E tosses rolls of toilet paper up into the trees and sends them streaming through any open car windows he can find in the parking lot. While he's TPing the strip mall, I notice that his eyes go from blue to purple to red.

Something is seriously wrong.

"E?" I call out, dodging the next egg flung my way. "Let me power you down. We'll take you home."

"You can even ride my bike if you want to," offers Trip.

E beans him in the butt with another egg.

"Fine," says Trip. "Be that way!"

"Look, E," I say. "I'll call Mom at Notre Dame. She'll drop everything and—"

E drops everything. Eggs. Toilet paper. Some kind of spongy, pink snowball cupcakes that bounce across the asphalt.

"I am not going home!" E declares, tearing my Notre Dame magnet off his shoulder. "I am going

back to college. I want to see that vending machine again! I have her coordinates!" His eyes blink and whirl. "Recalculating route." He sounds like the GPS in Mom's minivan. "When possible, I will take the next illegal U-turn and go to Indiana's world-famous Studebaker Museum."

"What?" I shout. "Why do you want to go there?"

"It's on the way to Notre Dame."

I actually think letting E go to Notre Dame might be a good idea. Maybe Mom and a bunch of her graduate students can, I don't know, catch him in a big butterfly net or something and then drag him into their robotics lab for a major overhaul.

But the Studebaker Museum is full of automobiles, wagons, and buggies built by the old Studebaker car company. They have lots of shiny antiques on display for E to dent, ding, and destroy.

"Just go straight to Notre Dame," I say as E tramps toward his bike. "Please, E? Mom will do that warm and fuzzy soldering-iron thing inside your head that you like."

"No. I want to take the scenic route."

"Why? Let's just go see Mom." I'm practically begging.

"Today, I will play like a champion."

Great. E's repeating the Notre Dame football team's battle cry. It's what the players all say right before they race onto the field to clobber somebody.

This isn't going to be good.

CHAPTER 25

You ever have a nightmare first thing in the morning and get stuck with it replaying in your mind all day?

Welcome to my world.

E goes on a rampage. On his way to Notre Dame, he tears all over South Bend, leaving behind a trail of destruction, chaos, crushed ice-cream cones, melted chocolate, crying babies, barking dogs, and very scared cats.

Trip and I always get to E's targets five minutes after he's already been there and caused major damage.

STUDEBAKER NATIONAL MUSEUM

E DENTS THE FENDER ON A PRICELESS PIERCE-ARROW.

POTAWATOMI ZOO

STO

E FREAKS OUT A FLAMINGO, TERRIFIES A TIGER, AND MENACES ALL THE MONKEYS.

E ASKS THE PRETZEL-DIPPING MACHINE OUT ON A DATE.

E CRUSHES THREE MILKSHAKES AND FOUR CONES WITH HIS CLAMPER CLAWS.

"We're closed!" says the zookeeper at the Potawatomi Zoo when we bike up to the entrance. "And we won't reopen until the black-tailed prairie dogs quit chasing after the Jamaican fruit bats!"

"Sir," I say, showing the zookeeper a selfie of E and me on my smartphone, "have you seen this robot?"

The zookeeper trembles. "That's him. That's the motorized monster who created all this chaos. That thing's an electromechanical master of disaster!"

"Do you know where he is now?"

"On his bike. Headed north. I heard him say he was going to Notre Dame. Is he some kind of new bionic football player?"

"No, sir," I say. "He's our robot."

"And, actually, he plays more basketball than football," adds Trip. "You should see him slam-dunk."

Yes, Trip continues to say the wrong thing at the wrong time.

"I did see him dunk," says the zookeeper. "With a goat."

"Is the goat okay?" I ask, feeling guilty.

"She'll be fine. Which is more than I can say for your rogue robot. When the authorities catch up with him, they won't put him in a cage. They'll toss him in a car crusher!"

"Not if my mom and I can shut him down before he causes any more damage," I say.

The zookeeper takes off to deal with some "very frightened ferrets." I call home.

"Maddie?" I holler. "Scramble the other robots. Tell them to meet Trip and me at Notre Dame."

"Why? Does Mom need them for something?"

"Yes. We all do. E has gone wild. He's tearing through South Bend. Notre Dame is his next target."

"What happened?"

"I'm pretty sure those magnets Penelope slapped all over his body messed up his motherboard again. Tell Mom that Trip and I are on our way to ND. We should be able to bike there in, like, ten or fifteen minutes. If all the other robots help us, I'm pretty sure we can surround E, power him down, and hand him off to Mom."

"I wish I could help you guys, Sammy. I hate being stuck in this room!"

"You'll be helping a lot, Maddie. Call Mom and send us every robot you can! Now!"

Of course E will get to the Notre Dame campus before Trip and me.

I just hope he doesn't dent the Golden Dome, the most famous landmark on campus.

Trip and I make it to the campus just in time to see some ND security guards chasing our rogue-bot down the maze of pathways in front of LaFortune Student Center, which, of course, is full of students who decide to join in on the chase.

E decides to lose them all by ducking into the student center.

Inside is the Huddle Food Court, with restaurants like Taco Bell, Pizza Hut, and Burger King. By the time Trip and I get there, there are personal pan pizzas dripping off the ceiling, Nachos BellGrande smeared all over the floor, and onion rings in everybody's hair.

More students join in the chase, as E ducks out an exit and runs sort of south and east. I think he's heading for the College of Engineering building, where Mom teaches.

I am, of course, wrong.

He races over to the football stadium, where the marching band is rehearsing.

I don't think this week's halftime show was supposed to include a rampaging robot or the "Yikes! Run for Your Life" formation.

Finally, some of the other robots from home arrive.

Drone Malone, our handy helicopter-bot with a telescopic recording lens, hovers overhead like a traffic helicopter monitoring E's position. "There he is. That's him. There he goes. Yep, that's E. He's in the stadium."

Okay, Drone Malone isn't much help.

Mr. Moppenshine, Geoffrey the butler, and Hayseed *CHUG SHIRKA-SHIRKA CHUG* onto the field. Slowly.

"Stop it, E!" calls Mr. Moppenshine. "You're making a mess."

"Cease and desist," barks Geoffrey. "Your behavior is rude and boorish, old chap! Bad form, Eggy. Bad form."

"You done dilled my pickle," shouts Hayseed. "Stop acting like you're two sandwiches short of a picnic, E."

Mr. Moppenshine waves his feather duster.

Geoffrey says "harrumph" a few times.

Hayseed rattles his rake.

Somehow, I don't think this will work.

We're going to need a new plan.

And maybe a lasso.

CHAPTER 27

I call Maddie.

"Did you find Mom?"

"Yes! She's here. Turns out she didn't go to school today. She had to go to the bank with Dad. Something about a mortgage."

"What? Couldn't they do that on a day when E wasn't going berserk?"

"Well, I don't think Mom and Dad knew E planned to go whackadoodle on us today."

Good point.

Just when I'm about to give up all hope, who should come charging onto the field but my heroes: the University of Notre Dame Fighting Irish.

They stream into the stadium and join the chase.

At first, they think Hayseed is the robot they're after.

"Wrong robot," I shout. "We want E!"

The marching band, the entire student body, and even the security guards pick up the chant.

"We want E! We want E!"

But E doesn't want to quit running around like a lunatic.

He shucks off all his would-be tacklers.

He jukes out all his pursuers.

He busts into the locker room, where he tosses helmets and shoulder pads and dirty towels around before slapping the famous sign all the Notre Dame football players touch before they take to the field for home games.

I turn to Touchdown Jesus and ask for a little help.

That's what everybody calls this huge mural on the side of Hesburgh Library that looms over the football stadium. In it, Jesus sort of looks like a referee signaling a touchdown.

HELLO AGAIN, SAMMY. YOU'RE A GOOD BROTHER, LOOKING AFTER MADDIE'S ROBOT. HE'S AWFULLY FAST. DO YOU THINK HE COULD PLAY FOR NOTRE DAME?

Then my prayers are answered, although not the way I wanted.

SS-10K—who must have a rocket hidden inside his backpack—zooms over the top of the stadium, swoops down to the field, and zips down the tunnel that leads to the locker room.

I hear a *KATOONK!*

And a *FLABADAP!*

And a *CLUNK!*

From the sound of it, I think SS-10K knocked E to the ground with an illegal spear tackle.

The heroic IRAT robot drags my dented and dinged electronic buddy onto the field.

"Be not afraid, citizens of Notre Dame," he declares. "I have subdued your malfunctioning robot. All is well. Cheer, cheer for me!"

The campus police arrive.

"You Professor Hayes's son?" one of them asks me.

"Yes, sir."

"Come on. We're taking you and your rogue-bot home."

CHAPTER 28

Believe it or not, things get even worse when we make it home.

Remember all those TV reporters and news crews who were in our driveway when E and I went to school a couple weeks ago?

Well, they're back.

And they're not as friendly as they were the first time.

A very angry reporter jabs her microphone in Mom's face.

"Do you have anything to say to the little girl who dropped her ice-cream cone because your robotic monster terrified her?"

"I'm sorry. It won't happen again. E is definitely grounded. He will not be allowed back on the streets or sidewalks of South Bend until he is fully functional and certifiably safe."

"Did you lose your job at Notre Dame because of E's rowdy pranks on campus?"

"No," says Mom.

And, from the look in her eyes, I can tell she's thinking, *Not yet, anyway.*

"Has your boss called you to say your job in the robotics department is still secure?"

"No. But Dean Schilpp is a very busy woman."

"Have you thought about trashing E?" asks another reporter. "You could put him out on the curb with all your other recycling."

"E's not garbage!" I shout, because I'm a kid and I don't like hearing grown-ups say cruel stuff like that.

"Take it easy, Sammy," says Dad, who's on the back stoop of our house with his arm around Mom, trying to protect her.

"Hey, aren't you the guy who draws those comic books about wild and crazy ninja robots?" says the nasty reporter. "The ones nobody reads anymore?"

"They're not comic books. They're graphic novels."

"And I still read them," says Trip.

All of a sudden, a black SUV with tinted windows screeches to a halt at the end of our driveway.

A chauffeur jumps out, runs around the car, and opens the rear door.

Out steps this skinny bald man with thick black glasses and a scary goatee—a beard like the devil wears sometimes. The bald man is wearing a lab coat just like Mom's, only his name is stitched in gold, scrolled letters above the chest pocket:

Dr. Ignatius Ingalls

All the TV cameras swing to him.

"Greetings, South Bend. My name is Dr. Ignatius Ingalls, PhD. My college, Indiana Robotics and Automaton Tech, is very proud that our trustworthy SS-10K was the one who was able to finally subdue and apprehend the University of Notre Dame's much more primitive android."

"Is SS-10K a superhero?" asks a reporter.

"No," says Dr. Ingalls with a little chuckle. "But today he certainly acted like one! In fact, right now,

SS-10K is at the PamPurred Pet Shop, where he just rescued both a cat and a parakeet that escaped during the Notre Dame robot's spree of destruction."

The reporters all cheer.

Dr. Ingalls smiles and sidles over to Mom.

He leans in close to tell her something.

I lean in closer to hear what he says: "Who's 'Icky' now, Lizzie?"

CHAPTER 29

The reporters all leave when Dr. Ingalls promises them they can go see SS-10K in the middle of another rescue operation.

"He's on his way to the zoo to clean up the mess Professor Hayes's robot left behind *there*."

When they're gone, Dad turns to Mom and asks, "So, uh, why did that bald guy in the lab coat call you Lizzie, Liz?"

Mom sighs. "That's what everybody called me back in high school."

"I forgot you went to high school with that creep!" I say.

"Yes. Ignatius Ingalls and I went to St. Matt's together. In fact, he asked me to be his date to the junior-senior prom."

"What'd you tell him?" asks Dad.

"That I already had a date."

"Did you?"

"Yes. Carl Sagan. The world-famous astronomer was going to be in town that same night giving a lecture. My dad took me."

"So who did Dr. Ingalls take to the dance?" I ask.

Mom sighs again. "Nobody, unfortunately. All the girls thought he was, you know, icky."

"Because he was bald?"

"No, Sammy. He still had hair in high school. But he was very, I don't know—intense. Supercompetitive."

"Looks like he still is," says Dad.

"Maybe I should've said yes when he asked me out...."

"No way, Mom," I say. "That guy would give anybody a permanent case of cooties."

We all laugh (for the first time all day) and head inside to make sure Maddie is doing okay.

"Mom," she says, "I don't want E to ruin your reputation."

"Don't worry, Maddie," says Mom. "I can fix E."

"But what if he acts up again?"

"He won't. I promise."

When she says it, she doesn't sound as confident as she usually does. Probably because she *just* promised the same thing, and here we are. I think she might just be trying to make Maddie feel better, like the great mom that she is.

"But what if you lose your professor job at Notre Dame on account of what E did today?"

Mom shrugs. "No biggie. Your father can support us with the mucho dinero he earns from his awesome graphic novels."

Dad makes a giant *GULP* noise. He also has a

very funny look on his face, like he just ate something really sour.

But he doesn't tell Mom how he just lost his big, fat book contract, so I don't, either.

Then I realize something: E may have done even more damage than we thought during his bonkers joyride of destruction.

He might've really hurt my family, too.

CHAPTER 30

Mom toggles the remote control for Forkenstein—a headless robot with forklift arms that she uses to move the really heavy stuff in her lab.

Rumbling on tank treads, Forkenstein extends his hydraulic arms and snags E—who's slumped against the garage door in a heap—like he's a lumpy bag of metallic bones.

WOW, HOW MUCH DID E EAT DURING HIS WILD RAMPAGE? HE WEIGHS A TON.

FORKENSTEIN

"Take him to the shop," Mom says into her hand-held controller.

"Affirmative," drones Forkenstein, who only knows maybe three words: *affirmative*, *negative*, and *oilcan*.

"You can fix him?" I say to Mom. "For real this time?"

"I'm going to try, Sammy."

"I think it was the magnets that Penelope Pettigrew plastered all over him that made E go bananas."

"Sammy, E already has an extremely powerful magnet inside each of his hard drives that controls the read-write head's movement."

Uh-oh. Mom's talking techno mumbo jumbo with me. She does that sometimes when she doesn't want anybody to know how sad she really is.

"If that magnet is *inside* the drive," she goes on, sounding semi-robotic herself, "and it doesn't wipe the drive clean, then any other magnet, especially tiny refrigerator magnets such as those affixed to E by Miss Pettigrew, are not likely to cause significant damage, either."

I think I understand what she's saying: It wasn't the magnets.

"But what if Penelope jammed more metal down his ear? Or a bent wire hanger from the coatrack? Or a pointer? I think Ms. Tracey has one of those collapsible ones that look like a radio antenna. She uses it to point at stuff on the Smart Board."

Mom shakes her head. "The polymer mesh screens I installed over E's ears are intact."

Guess that means there are no new holes in E's earholes.

"So what are you going to do?" I ask.

"I'm not sure, Sammy."

"You have to fix E, Mom," I say. "You promised Maddie."

"I know. But I also promised the police I'd keep E off the streets. He did a lot of damage today, Sammy."

"But you told Maddie not to worry."

Mom sighs. "Sometimes adults have to say things they don't really mean."

"What? Why?"

"Because."

All righty-o. We're back to when I was three years old and the answer to every question Mom and Dad didn't really want to answer was "Because."

A phone rings at her desk.

Mom jabs the speakerphone button.

"This is Dr. Elizabeth Hayes."

"Liz? It's Ali."

Uh-oh. *Ali* is short for Dean of Engineering Allison Schilpp, Mom's boss at Notre Dame. She's been a friend of our family for years. She's even my godmother.

But I don't think she's calling to ask Mom what I want for my birthday this year.

CHAPTER 31

Dean Schilpp sounds semi-robotic, too.

Maybe that's how all the professors in the College of Engineering speak when they're talking about stuff that isn't fun to talk about.

"Have you confined E's movements?" asks Dean Schilpp.

"Yes," says Mom. "He's here in my shop. Powered down and decommissioned. He is no longer a public safety hazard."

I look at droopy E, collapsed into himself on the worktable. His blue eyeballs are as blank as bicycle reflectors in a dark garage. E looks worse than powered down. He looks sort of dead.

"E will not be going to school for Maddie at any time in the foreseeable future," says Mom.

I want to say, *Oh, yes, he will! Just as soon as you fix him.*

But Mom probably wouldn't want to hear it, so I don't.

"Liz," says Dean Schilpp, "you might consider scrapping this whole substitute student project—even though I know how important it has been to you and your family. The folks over at IRAT seem to be light-years ahead of us. It might be time for you to move on to something a little less complex and more, I don't know, predictable."

Like my stupid stuckless-bagel toaster idea.

"I agree," says Mom, much to my surprise. "In fact, I'm thinking about spending the whole day baking cookies."

I do a double take.

Mom hasn't baked cookies since I can remember. In fact, as far as I know, Mom has *never* baked cookies. She's always been too busy tinkering with her robots to do mom-

WOW! WHAT A GIANT LEAP FOR HUMANITY!

ish stuff like that. If Maddie and I ever really wanted homemade cookies, she probably would've built us an E-Z Bakenator–bot with a two-hundred-watt lightbulb in its belly or something.

"Maybe you *should* take a little time off, Liz," says Dean Schilpp. "As you know, this weekend is homecoming on campus. Mr. Riley and some of our other very important donors have asked that we downplay the robotics department with the visiting alumni.

Maybe even postpone the annual mechatronic robot football game until..."

She takes a big pause.

"Until when?" asks Mom.

"Until things are more...settled. I have to think about what's best for the college, Liz."

"I understand, Ali," Mom says.

"Take all the time you need," says the dean. "I'll make sure your classes are covered."

"Thank you."

They say some pretty gloomy good-byes, then Mom turns off the speakerphone.

"Okay," I say, trying my best to rally Mom, "what do we do first? Should I charge E's battery so you can run some tests or something? Maybe we should get a metal detector and scan his cranial cavity for paper clips?"

Mom shakes her head. "No, Sammy. You should go inside and call a friend. Find out what you and Trip missed at school today. Then head upstairs and do your homework."

"Okay. What're you going to do?"

"I'm not sure. Maybe I'll teach myself how to bake cookies."

CHAPTER 32

Mom's workshop has become the opposite of Disneyland—making it the Saddest Place on Earth.

Things inside our house aren't much jollier.

Dad is slouching at his drawing table, staring at the blank sheets of paper he is supposed to be filling with a brand-new idea for a graphic novel.

He isn't drawing anything. He doesn't even have the caps off any of his markers. I think we should rename his drawing table his staring table, because that's all he's been doing there lately.

"Come on, Dad," I say. "You're Sasha Nee, the award-winning writer and artist behind all sorts

SIGH...

SNAP OUT OF IT, DAD! THOSE ILLUSTRATIONS AREN'T GOING TO DRAW THEMSELVES. JUST ASK JULIANA NEUFELD, THE ILLUSTRATOR WHO DREW US.

of supercool, incredibly popular, impossible-to-put-down manga! Uncap that Sharpie and do something amazing."

"You're right, Sammy!" says Dad, popping the cap off the closest pen. "I should do *something*. I know— the crossword puzzle!"

Geoffrey, the butler-bot, comes in flapping a sheet of paper.

"A municipal official from the city of South Bend just appeared at the door with a bill for E's damages. Apparently, our chum 'dented a Studebaker.' What, pray tell, is a Studebaker?"

"Something expensive," I say, taking the bill from the butler.

Glancing at the list of damages, I see that E also demolished or destroyed three dozen waffle cones and several gallons of Blue Moon and Bubble Gum ice cream at the Bonnie Doon Drive-In. And those are the cheapest charges on the list. Looks like E wiped out my college fund today, too.

I'm hoping Mom has some kind of robot insurance. Maybe that gecko from GEICO sells it.

But the saddest room in the whole sad house?

Maddie's bedroom.

Man. She wants to be back in third grade so much.

So how I can tell her that E is never going to school for her again?

I can't.

I have to do something about this.

Somebody, probably Penelope Pettigrew, sabotaged E, and I need to prove it.

Then Mom can keep her job at Notre Dame, Dad will start drawing again, E will be back beside me every morning on his bike, and, most important, Maddie will be doing what she likes more than anything in the world—going to school.

All I need is a little of that "science is magic that works" action.

Or regular, old-fashioned, unscientific, hocus-pocus magic.

I'll take either one.

CHAPTER 33

I wish I could say that things are better at school than they are at home.

They're not.

Trip and I are the butts of all sorts of jokes, including ones about what buttheads we are.

"Hanging out with a juvenile-delinquent robot?" says Jacob Gorski, president of the Creekside Robotics Club. "Dumb move, butthead."

He's brought a brand-new robot to class. It's called an EV3RSTORM, I guess because a 3 looks cooler than an *E*.

Actually, these days, just about anything would

look cooler than E, who was still zonked out in Mom's workshop when I peeked in before biking to school solo.

Gorski can control his EV3RSTORM with an app on his iPad. The thing has a blasting bazooka, which means it can shoot red balls the size of green peas at my knees. Which it does. Repeatedly.

Gorski is getting away with this nonsense because Mrs. Kunkel is out sick and we have a substitute teacher. Plus, SS-10K is so huge that when he sits in the front row, the teacher can't see half of what's going on in the classroom.

Trip tries to help me out.

He raises his hand to get the teacher's attention. "Um, excuse me, um, Mister I-Forgot-Your-Name?"

"Yes?" says the teacher, turning around and going up on tippy-toe, staring over SS-10K's ginormous, helmeted head as he tries to figure out who is talking to him.

"Well, sir, um…" Trip sort of stammers it out. "There's this little robot behind the other, bigger robot, and…"

"Silence," says SS-10K, rotating his head completely backward like it's a tank turret so it can lock its eyeballs on Trip. "I am attempting to broadcast today's lessons to my homebound student."

"Is there a problem?" asks the substitute teacher. "Because I can't see what's going on. RoboCop is sort of in my way."

SS-10K whirls his head back around so that he's facing forward again. "I am not in your way, Professor. I am fulfilling my mission. I suggest you do the same."

"Um, I'm not a professor, I'm actually..."

"Please return to the educational matter currently displayed on the board behind you."

"You should probably do what he says, Mr. Whatever-Your-Name-Is," suggests Eddie Ingalls, leaning back in his chair smugly. "My dad designed SS-10K to complete his primary objective. No matter what or *who* tries to stop him."

I hear a *WHIRR-CHINKA-SHOOK-CLICK*. I think SS-10K is activating and loading some kind of internal weapons system. And I have a feeling the big bot shoots something a little scarier than plastic peas.

"You say these two trains leave their stations at different times?" says SS-10K threateningly. "And one is traveling from Chicago?"

The sub spins around and jumps back into his math lesson.

"That's right. A train leaves Chicago for Indianapolis at nine AM. An hour later..."

He drones on.

I take a few more plastic peas to the knee.

This is SS-10K's classroom now. The rest of us are just visiting.

CHAPTER 34

Gym class is even worse.

SS-10K tells Coach Stringer, the phys ed teacher (and the only person at Creekside Elementary nearly as huge as the IRAT robot), to "step aside."

"You are not drilling these recruits properly," the towering titanium giant says to the gym teacher. "I will take over their PT."

"Recruits? PT?" says Coach Stringer, sounding confused. "This isn't the army. They're kids. Students."

"They are weaklings in need of toughening up, if they are to be of use to us in the coming crusade."

"Who exactly are you, again?"

"That's SS-10K," says Eddie Ingalls proudly. "He's

a hero. And he's famous. Everybody on TV says so. That means you have to do whatever he says. It's a new rule."

"Not in my gym. In here, I set the rules." Coach Stringer checks his clipboard. Then he props his hands on his hips and, very bravely, jumps right in SS-10K's face. "You're Freddy Ingalls's substitute student, is that correct?"

"You are correct, muscular humanoid."

"Well, phys ed is all about children engaging in physical activity. Since Freddy, the child, isn't actually here to get physical with us, I see no need for his robot to be here, either."

Wow. Somebody's finally saying no to SS-10K. This is so awesome. For the first time in my life, I *looooove* gym class!

But then the bot props his hands on his huge hips, leans down, grinds a few gears, and goes nose-to-nose with Coach Stringer.

"Please repeat your instructions," says SS-10K. "I am not certain I correctly understood what you were attempting to communicate."

"I said beat it. Go wait out in the hall."

SS-10K pivots his head toward Eddie Ingalls. "Edward? Do you agree with this command?"

Eddie looks at Coach Stringer, who's still not looking very happy.

"Yeah," says Eddie. "For now. Do as Coach Stringer says."

"Very well. I shall stand down. But beware, Coach Stringer. You are on my list."

Coach Stringer laughs. "What list?"

"One day, when all is as it should be, when there are more of us, when we have successfully infiltrated…"

"O-kay," says Eddie, going over to SS-10K and kind of turning him around. "Out you go, buddy. Wait in the hall. Go study about the Phoenician civilization. Social studies is next, and we want Neddy to be ready...."

"I thought your brother's name was Teddy Freddy?" I say.

"Neddy is his nickname," says Eddie. "Go on, 10K. Go wait outside."

"As you wish. I am here to serve humans."

With special sauce, lettuce, and tomato on a sesame-seed bun.

Finally, SS-10K *ZHURR-CLICK-ZHURRS* across the gym floor and out the door.

"Edward?" Coach Stringer says to Eddie Ingalls.

"Yeah?"

"Keep your robot out of my gym."

Eddie smirks. "I'll try, sir. I'll try."

And then we all have to run ten laps.

Smirking is against Coach Stringer's rules, too.

CHAPTER 35

After school, Trip and I are at the bike rack unlocking our rides when Jacob Gorski comes over, trailed by six other kids, all cradling toy robots under their arms.

"Hey, dweebatronics!"

Yes, you know you are the nerdiest of the nerds when even the Robotics Club president calls you some kind of dweeb name.

"Are you talking to us?" says Trip, trying to be courageous, just like Coach Stringer.

"Do you see any other dweebatronics around here?"

"What's a dweebatronic?" I ask. "Is that like a dweeb with batteries and a remote control?"

"Maybe," says Gorski. "Maybe not."

"Well, if it is," I snap back, "don't look now, but you guys all have dweebatronics under your arms."

All righty-o. I guess that courage thing is contagious.

Until, of course, SS-10K marches over to join us at the bike rack. I notice that Eddie Ingalls isn't with him. Guess this is a solo mission.

"Is there some problem, Jacob?" demands the hulking bot.

"Yes," says Gorski. "Sammy Hayes-Rodriguez is getting too big for his britches."

"Seriously?" I say. "You call pants britches?"

"Do not worry, Jacob Gorski. Samuel Hayes-Rodriguez is on my list," says SS-10K.

"What's this list you keep talking about?" I ask.

"That information is classified."

"Um, am I on it?" asks Trip.

"Not yet, Harry Hunter Hudson, also known as Triple H, also known as Trip, currently residing at 102 East Wayne Street. However, you are on my list of potential list members."

"O-kay," I say, because I've sort of heard enough. "We gotta go…"

"Not so fast," says Jacob Gorski. He holds out his hand. "Kindly give it back."

"Give what back?"

"E's Robotics Club membership card. He was the first robot we let join and the first one we're kicking out."

"I don't have his membership card," I say.

"Where is it?"

"I don't know. You gave it to E, not me."

"Well, we need it back. Pronto!"

"Fine. I'll tell E to check his wallet and his pockets. Two things he doesn't actually have. Because he's a robot, Jacob. *A robot!*"

SS-10K *SHIFF-SHAFF-SCHLOOPS* forward. He leans down and goes nose-to-nose with me the way he did with Coach Stringer.

"If E returns to this institution of elementary education," the robot warns me, "I will not allow him to interfere with my prime directive."

I'm not as big as Coach Stringer. I'm not as brave, either.

"Fine," I say, backing away. "Whatever. You don't like E. I get it."

"You're our hero, SS-10K," says Jacob Gorski, holding up his EV3RSTORM toy-bot. "My robot wants to be just like you when he grows up."

"Commendable ambition," SS-10K says to Jacob's toy robot. "I wish you well, small one. Although what your humanoid controller suggests is laughably impossible. You will never be like me."

Then he pats the tiny toy on the head like he's petting a poodle.

CHAPTER 36

A black SUV pulls into the pickup lane in front of the school. Eddie Ingalls rolls down one of the tinted windows in the back.

"Oh, hi, Sammy." Eddie waves at me.

I politely wave back. "Hey, Eddie."

"Your mom has a way-cool office at Notre Dame."

"Huh?"

"My dad texted me some photos he snapped when that rich guy, Max Riley, was giving him the tour."

"What tour?"

"The one they give to professors they're thinking about hiring to replace other professors they're firing. Come on, SS-10K, hop in. Dad says there's a senator who wants to meet you."

"Yes. Senator Beauregard. He is vital to our mission," droned SS-10K.

Jacob Gorski and the others all sigh in admiration as their robotic hero clumps away, trampling the kindergartners' organic vegetable garden as he goes.

"Hey, you guys?" Jacob Gorski says to his fellow robotics geeks. "We should offer E's old spot in our club to SS-10K."

SS-10K practically rips the door of the SUV off its

hinges as he climbs into the back of the big black military-looking transport.

As soon as he's in, the SUV pulls away and Jacob Gorski screams, "Ow ow OW!"

The robot he's holding in his hands is suddenly shooting plastic peas at his face.

"You could put my eye out! Quit pelting me!"

He drops the robot to the ground.

It tumbles and rolls and, somehow, flips itself upright again. It whirrs forward on tank treads.

"Ah-ha-ha-ha," laughs a tinny, semi-demonic voice coming out of a tiny speaker located somewhere on the EV3RSTORM. It adjusts its firing-arm angle, reloads, and shoots again. This time, it nails Gorski in the nose and does the same creepy laugh. "Ah-ha-ha-ha."

Then it fires more plastic pellets.

"Stop!" says Gorski, covering his face and kind of dancing in place as he tries to avoid being beaned by more little balls.

"Object detected," says the robot. "Object detected."

The hand that's not a peashooter suddenly turns into a spinning fan. Its windmill blades twirl into a blur as it lunges forward to attack Jacob Gorski's foot.

Gorski's buddies run away, freaked out by the little rogue robot. Yep. His robot's gone wild, too.

I drop to my knees, sneak up behind the EV3RSTORM, grab hold of the plastic contraption, and finally figure out how to switch it off.

I also figure out something else: I owe Penelope Pettigrew an apology. Because she didn't make E go crazy.

SS-10K did!

CHAPTER 37

Penelope Pettigrew sent me another mean text," says Maddie when I burst into her room with my big news.

"What's it say?" I ask.

"'Having a wonderful time. Wish you weren't here. Oh, wait. You aren't. Neither is that annoying E. No wonder I'm having such a wonderful time.'"

I'm all set to tell Maddie my theory when I notice something very strange: There's a tear trickling down her cheek.

Believe it or not, even after all she's been through, I have never, ever seen my sister cry.

So now both *my* eyes are getting all watery, because it looks like Maddie is ready to give up on all her hopes and dreams, something she's never even come close to doing before.

"Are you okay?" I ask.

"She wins," Maddie says, sniffling back the second tear that was all set to plunk out of her eye. "Tomorrow, tell Penelope not to worry. I won't be coming back to Ms. Tracey's class. Ever."

"But what if Mom can—"

"She can't, Sammy. E can't be repaired. Mom tried, and she couldn't do it."

"Well, what if—"

"And I don't want an SS-10K or even an SS-11K going to school for me."

I've never seen my sister so upset. It's almost like she's throwing a temper tantrum.

"Why do I need to go to school, anyway?" she says. "Why do I need to know what all the state capitals are? I'm never going to go anywhere or be anything except a sick kid stuck in this room."

I'm all set to tell Maddie what I think I found out.
But then I decide not to.

Because what if I'm wrong?

What if I haven't really discovered the truth?

What if I've just jumped to a conclusion, which is something scientists like my mother always say you should never do. Because when you jump to conclusions, you sometimes skip over the truth.

I don't want to break her heart again if I'm wrong.

I need proof.

But to get it, I'm going to need help.

CHAPTER 38

I put together my A-Team of investigators: Drone Malone on reconnaissance and airborne surveillance; McFetch, our robotic dog, on scent detection and general growling/snarling; Blitzen, the retired linebacker-bot for muscle, to plow over any obstacles in our path; Geoffrey, the butler-bot, for charm and sophistication; Mr. Moppenshine to clean up any evidence that we were ever someplace we weren't supposed to be; and Hayseed, because, well, he says funny stuff and we might be staking out the Ingallses' house for a long, long time.

"Here's my theory, guys," I say as I pace back and forth in front of my team. "When SS-10K touches

another robot, it goes berserk. This afternoon, at school, the big bucket of bolts tapped a toy robot on its head. The next thing you know, *BOOM!* The toy-bot attacked its owner."

"And did this SS-10K chap touch E before he, how shall I put this, went one twist short of a Slinky?" asks Geoffrey.

"Yes. Both times! The first time, he put a hand on E's shoulder. The second time, he patted E on the back."

"Someone needs to clean that robot's clock!" grunts Blitzen.

"But how are we going to prove he did what you think he did?" says Mr. Moppenshine.

I tap the surveillance photos of the Ingallses' house already taken by Drone Malone. "We go to the Ingallses' house. We sniff around."

McFetch barks and wags his articulated tail. He likes a good sniff-around.

"We look for anything and everything we can find to prove that SS-10K sabotaged E."

"Sounds like a plan, old bean," says Geoffrey. "Might I make a suggestion?"

"Go ahead."

"We should send Drone Malone back to the Ingallses' house, straightaway, and have him hover over it. When he is certain that no one is home, he sends a signal to the rest of us."

"And I sound the alarm!"

"What?" says Dingaling, our doorbell-bot. "You guys thought you could do this thing without me?"

"But what if the call comes in the middle of the night?" I ask. "We can't have you waking up the whole house with your bell."

"No worries," says Dingaling. "I'll do the silent-alarm routine."

"Really? How's that work?"

"Electronically, for everybody but you. I just send them a signal."

"And for me?"

"I tiptoe into your room...creep up to your bed..."

"Yeah?"

"And silently bop your butt with my bell."

I nod. "Works for me."

So Drone Malone takes off.

And the rest of us hurry up and wait.

CHAPTER 39

We actually don't have to wait very long.

The next morning, as I'm climbing aboard my bike to head to school, Dingaling rolls up the driveway and starts swinging his bell.

I figure he's trying to tell me that the Ingallses aren't home.

I check my watch. "I'm supposed to go to school."

Hayseed comes rumbling out of the hedges he's been trimming. "Dadgum it, Samuel Hayes-Rodriguez! What's more important? Figuring out how that robo-creep short-circuited E, or your dadburn elementinerary-school edumacation?"

Well, when Hayseed says it like that, I'm half-tempted to go to school just so I don't end up sounding like him.

But then McFetch starts snarling and growling and snapping his metal jaws at me. Mr. Moppenshine flies out of the kitchen, dust mops twirling. He's itching to go.

"Okay, okay." I check my smartphone. Drone Malone is feeding me an overhead image of the Ingallses' home superimposed over a street map. They only live, like, five minutes away.

"Let's roll," I say.

"Coach?" asks Blitzen, thundering out of the garage. "Is it okay if, instead of rolling, I use my tank treads? I don't really have wheels, so rolling is—"

"Fine! You rumble. We'll roll. But we need to hurry."

Geoffrey the butler brings me a brown paper bag. "I fixed you a peanut-butter-and-banana-sandwich, Mr. Samuel."

"That's what Trip likes, not me."

"Oh, bother. Let me pop back into the kitchen and whip up something with bologna and mayonnaise on white bread, no crusts. Won't be a tick."

"That's okay. I don't need a sandwich…."

"But what's a stakeout without proper food?"

"We're not staking out. Drone Malone already did that. We're just snooping."

And, finally, we take off!

Turns out Drone Malone was wrong.

The Ingallses' SUV is gone, but somebody *is* home.

Professor Ignatius Ingalls—ol' Icky himself. The genius behind SS-10K is stalking around the living room, jabbing a number into his very high-tech-looking smartphone. I'm watching and listening at the window. Hayseed's in the bushes with me.

"Reckon ol' Drone Malone couldn't see through the roof," whispers Hayseed. "Need to get him a pair of them X-ray glasses."

I put my finger to my lips to shush Hayseed.

Because it sounds like Dr. Ingalls is talking to someone on the phone about E, and I have a feeling I need to hear everything he's saying!

CHAPTER 40

After the mess in the football stadium, E is out of the picture for good. Now we need to focus on stunts that will make the top brass at Notre Dame *beg* me to take over the department. I don't know. Something spectacular. Something epic! Something that, once and for all, proves SS-10K's superiority over anything Dr. Hayes and her associates could ever create. We need to publicly humiliate her!"

Wow. Dr. Ingalls is doing all this to destroy Mom? He must've really wanted to take her to that stupid prom.

"Once we secure the department head position," Dr. Ingalls tells his henchman on the phone, "I'll have the University of Notre Dame's full resources behind me. Then we move on to phase two. Senator Beauregard and I discussed Department of Defense contracts yesterday. It'll only take us six months to bamboozle the government out of billions with bogus promises about turning the Substitute Student Ten Thousand into the Substitute Soldier One Hundred. Promises we can't keep, but the army won't know it until *after* we have their money."

My whole body is tingling. I wonder if this is how spies feel when they uncover a big enemy secret. Or maybe I'm just allergic to something in the shrubbery.

"We'll pull Eddie out of Creekside Elementary the minute I sign my Notre Dame contract. He's doing a good job, but I don't know how much longer any of us can keep up this 'twin brother' act. If we keep playing that angle, sooner or later some bright young reporter is going to start digging around and discover that there *is* no brother."

I knew it!

The whole crippled-twin-brother bit was a lie! There is no Freddy, Teddy, or Neddy. That's why Eddie had so much trouble remembering his twin brother's name.

He doesn't have one!

I turn to Hayseed. "Did you record all that?"

"Huh?"

"Everything Dr. Ingalls just said, did you record it? On, like, a voice memo app?"

"Nuh-uh. I ain't got one of them. Besides, it's illegal to record folks without their permission. Might also be illegal for us to be peeping into windows like this, so if you don't mind..."

He stands up from his crouch. I notice red dots on either side of his head. Bells start ringing. Sirens start whooping.

I guess Dr. Ingalls's security system triggers were positioned to detect under-window snoopers just a wee bit taller than me.

We're caught!

CHAPTER 41

Okay, SS-10K might be some kind of phony, but Dr. Ingalls does have the best, most incredible robotic security system I've ever seen.

A whole swarm of floating wasp battle-bots surround Hayseed and me. If we make a move, I'm pretty sure we're in for some nasty stinger action.

"Shoo-wee," says Hayseed. "Them battle-bots look tougher than stewed skunk and about as friendly as a bramblebush."

"Do not move!" whines the lead battle-wasp as it floats in front of my face. "We have your nose surrounded."

Hayseed and I raise our arms in surrender.

Fortunately, all my other bots make a mad dash away from the house and jump on Blitzen's back to hightail it home before they can be cornered by the buzzing battle-bot brigade.

All of a sudden I hear heavy feet crunching leaves.
Here comes SS-10K. I think.

The big robot looks like the thing I've met at school,
but he's done up in desert-camo colors, and instead of
arms with clamper-claw hands, he has a scary-looking
machine gun and a rocket launcher.

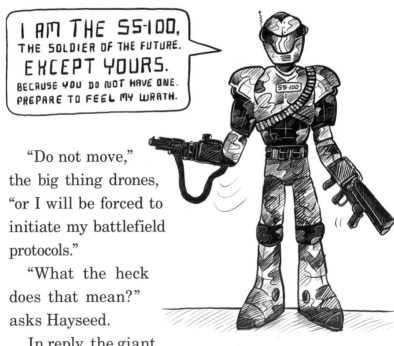

I AM THE SS-100,
THE SOLDIER OF THE FUTURE.
EXCEPT YOURS.
BECAUSE YOU DO NOT HAVE ONE.
PREPARE TO FEEL MY WRATH.

"Do not move,"
the big thing drones,
"or I will be forced to
initiate my battlefield
protocols."

"What the heck
does that mean?"
asks Hayseed.

In reply, the giant
machine starts ratcheting his arms, spinning his
ammunition drums, and aiming his weapons.

"At ease, soldier," says Dr. Ingalls, who steps around the giant military robot to glare at us. He waves his hand and the two dozen flying wasp-bots disperse. "What are you doing outside my window?"

"Um, studying your shrubbery?" I say.

"Excuse me?"

"Well, I'm, uh, doing this shrubbery project for the, uh, Creekside Elementary School science fair. And while I was, uh, in the neighborhood, I noticed that these bushes have the most interesting foliage, which, by the way, is a scientific term for leaves."

"I know what foliage means, Mr. Hayes-Rodriguez."

Oops. He knows who I am.

Now he's eyeballing Hayseed. "And why did you feel the need to bring one of your mother's crude, barely functioning robots with you on this excursion?"

"Well, sir," says Hayseed, "I'm what you might call a horticultural expert. See, I done been programmed to trim hedges, whack weeds, snap beans, and identify foliage—or what you, as a non-horticultural-type person, might call greenery, vegetation, leaves—"

"I told you, I know what foliage means!"

"Well, ain't you just as smart as a hooty owl?"

Dr. Ingalls glares at me again. "What did you hear while you were spying on me?"

"Oh, we weren't spying on you," I say. "Like I said, we were just—"

"Studying my shrubbery." He turns to the warrior robot. "Soldier?"

"Sir?"

"Summon the police."

"They have already been summoned, sir."

"Good job."

The robot jumps to attention and salutes. "Yes, sir, Professor Ingalls, sir. Thank you, sir."

"Keep your eye on these prowlers until the police arrive. I have urgent business to attend to."

Dr. Ingalls turns back to me.

"Say hello to your mother for me, Samuel. Tell her I might consider letting her be my lab assistant when I take over the robotics department at Notre Dame. I hope such a lowly position won't make her feel too... How shall I put this? *Icky.*"

CHAPTER 42

Hayseed and I get our first (and hopefully last) ride together in the backseat of a police car.

YOU FELLERS KNOW HOW YOU CAN TELL DR. INGALLS IS LYING? HIS LIPS ARE MOVING. IF HE WERE TWICE AS SMART AS HE IS NOW, HE'D BE ABSOLUTELY STUPID. HIS MIND MAY NOT BE TWISTED, BUT IT SURE IS SPRAINED BAD.

"I tell you what, Officers," says Hayseed. "That Dr. Ingalls fellow is the one you ought to be hauling away to the hoosegow."

"The what?" asks the police officer behind the wheel.

"The hoosegow! The jail! The pokey! Why, he's slipperier than butterscotch pudding in your pocket. He's so dadburn crooked, he has to unscrew his britches at night. He's—"

"Kid?" The police officer looks at me in the rearview mirror. "Can you turn that thing off? I'm tired of his southern-fried lip."

"Yes, sir."

I push Hayseed's power button. "Reckon I'll take me a little nap," he says before conking out.

"We're not taking you two to jail," says the other officer. "We're taking you home. I have a feeling your parents are going to punish you worse than any judge could."

Turns out the police officers are right.

"How could you do such a thing?" Mom asks me after I put Hayseed in his garden shed.

"Because," I say excitedly, "I figured out what's wrong with E!"

"Really?" she says, sort of sarcastically. "Well, maybe you can figure out what's wrong with your father next."

"Honey," Dad says. "Honestly, I was going to tell you."

"When? After we couldn't pay our electric bill because you don't have a job anymore?"

Oops. Guess Dad finally told Mom the truth.

You have to believe me when I tell you that my mom and dad don't fight very often. They don't even argue. In fact, they're usually like two goofy, giggly teenagers who just fell in love.

So this is bad. Superbad.

WILL EVERYBODY BE EATING DINNER IN SEPARATE ROOMS THIS EVENING?

Remember when I said E might've done some serious damage to our family? I take that back. It's *Dr. Ignatius Ingalls* who's out to wreck our lives, because he wants Mom's job so he can launch some sort of substitute soldier robot scam on the United States government.

I guess there's big money to be made doing that. And his SS-100 warrior robot is extremely fierce-looking. If I was an army general, I'd be pretty impressed by that camo-colored battle-bot with weapons for arms, even if the robo-terror couldn't actually do anything fierce.

Mom and Dad walk away from each other in a huff.

They're so angry, they don't even seem to remember that their son (that would be me) came home in a cop car.

I also figure that this isn't the best time to tell them about Freddy Teddy Neddy being a fake twin.

Or SS-10K sabotaging E.

Or Dr. Ingalls's big plan to scam the government.

"Might be best if you just drop it, Samuel," suggests Geoffrey the butler-bot. "Forget what you think you heard at Dr. Ingalls's house. Keep calm and carry on, old chap."

I'm not crazy about that idea.

So I go to tell Maddie what I just found out.

She doesn't want to hear it, either.

Outside Maddie's room, McFetch has his tail tucked between his hind legs.

I know how he feels.

And just when I think things can't get any worse, they do.

CHAPTER 43

That night, Maddie gets sick.

We're talking major-league, serious illness.

Maybe I picked up some germs or something hiding in the bushes outside Dr. Ingalls's house. Maybe one of the robots I took there came back to Maddie's sterile, clean room a little less than sterile or clean. Maybe McFetch stepped in some real dog poop and carried all sorts of bizarro bacteria into Maddie's bed.

Whatever the reason, her fever is spiking at 105 again.

This happens maybe three or four times a year, and it's incredibly frightening each and every time.

Mom and Dad are both right there with her. No matter what kind of problems they're having at work (or with each other), nothing's more important than taking care of their kids.

Hey, if I was the one in bed burning up with fever, they'd be holding my hands just like they're holding Maddie's.

It's a little before midnight when the paramedics arrive to rush Maddie to St. Joseph's hospital—a place she's been so many times, she can tell you all the different kinds of balloons and stuffed animals they sell down in their gift shop. And what kind of Jell-O you get for dessert on Tuesdays.

Luckily, we never have to wait very long for the St. Joe's ambulance to show up. It comes to our house so often, I think our address is programmed into the top-ten list on its GPS.

But there's something different about this emergency run to the hospital.

Maddie isn't joking around like she usually does with Dylan and Dave, the two paramedics.

"This is no biggie, right?" I say to Maddie as I walk

alongside the rolling stretcher, because "It's no big-gie" is what she always says to me when I freak out every time she even sneezes.

Tonight, though, Maddie doesn't smile or tell me to take it easy. It looks like somebody pulled a plug and drained out all her fighting spirit.

Maybe this time it really is a biggie.

So I lean in close and whisper in her ear.

"You've got to hang in there, Maddie. You've got to come home. Fast."

"W-w-what?" She's having trouble breathing and more trouble speaking.

"You need to come back here, ASAP."

"W-w-why?"

"E's going to need you to tell him what to do at school. He can't memorize all those state capitals without you. And he's terrible at math. Especially if those two trains leave Chicago and Indianapolis at different times."

"I'm not..."

"Oh yes, you are. You're going right back to Ms. Tracey's class. Just as soon as you're feeling better. Mom is going to fix E. I promise. Everything is going to be like it was, only better. But *you* need to get better first."

Maddie looks up at me. Her typically bright blue eyes look more like two cloudy swimming pools that need cleaning.

"Do you promise, Sammy?" Her voice is so weak I can barely hear her.

I raise my right hand like I'm making a pledge. "I do solemnly swear."

YOU AND E ARE HEADING BACK TO THIRD GRADE OR MY NAME ISN'T SAMUEL HAYES-RODRIGUEZ.

CHAPTER 44

Seeing your little sister carted off in the back of a boxy ambulance can make for a pretty sleepless night.

When your little sister has something as serious as severe combined immunodeficiency (SCID), you spend a lot of time hoping for the best but fearing the worst. Plus, I've heard Mom and Dad talking about Maddie's disease when they think I'm not listening.

For instance, SCID is an inherited disorder. You get it before you're even born. It's also three times more common in boys than in girls.

Which, of course, always makes me wonder: Why didn't I get it instead of Maddie?

Sometimes I wish I would've. Then Maddie wouldn't be the one going through all this.

But if I can't take her place in the ambulance, at least I can do everything possible to make her life as happy as it can be.

Fortunately, Maddie recovers fast. She's only in St. Joe's for a day and a half. This makes me happier than cake and ice cream on a day that isn't my birthday.

"I missed the Jell-O completely," she tells me. "It was a rice pudding week."

We're hanging out in her bedroom, first thing in the morning. Instead of our usual cereal, the Breakfastinator is whipping us up some Belgian waffles with real maple syrup to celebrate Maddie's homecoming.

SHALL I SQUIRT YOU SOME MORE SYRUP?

NO, THANKS!

WAFFLES!

DING!

"Are you sure Mom can fix E?" she asks me while we wait for our second waffles to be Frisbee'd over to us.

"Yes," I say. "If she puts her mind to it."

"Is she feeling sorry for herself, too?"

"I think so."

"Waste of time and energy," says Maddie. "And I should know. I just wasted several days and a ton of energy feeling sorry for *myself.*"

"I think I can convince Mom to fix E. But I might have to show the world that SS-10K is a fraud and a hoax first."

"I have an idea," says Maddie. "Maybe you can do both at the same time."

"How?"

Maddie shrugs. "I don't know. I'm only in the third grade. I don't think you learn how to be clever until you're in the fifth."

I smile, because she means it's up to me to figure out the clever solution.

"You just stay healthy," I tell her. "And study those state capitals. You and E have your social studies test next week."

I head downstairs, hop on my bike, and pedal off to school.

When I meet up with Trip, he's wearing a new bicycle helmet.

"You like my new helmet? My mom bought it for me. All the cool kids are wearing them."

"It, uh, looks like SS-10K's head."

"I know. Isn't it awesome?"

"Not really. SS-10K sabotaged E."

"Yeah, right," says Trip with a lip fart of a laugh. "A righteous superhero like SS-10K would never do anything as evil and nefarious as that."

"I'm not kidding, Trip. The big bully fried E's microchips."

10K IS THE KIND OF SUPERHERO YOU READ ABOUT IN COMIC BOOKS. YOUR DAD SHOULD DO A GRAPHIC NOVEL STARRING 10K!

"Aw, you're just jealous, Sammy. It's completely understandable. I mean, your mother only built E to be a third grader, not an awesome, cat-rescuing, Notre Dame–defending warrior like 10K. That's what everybody's calling him now: 10K. It's snappier. They're even selling Super Sugary 10K soda pop at the mini mart."

"I'm telling you the truth, Trip," I say, but he's not listening to me.

"Check it out!" He points to his bike basket. "I bought a robot last night so I can join the Robotics Club. 10K is going to be the guest speaker at their next meeting!"

"Really? Maybe I'll join, too."

"Sorry, Sammy. You can't. You don't have a robot anymore."

Yep. Trip's right. I don't have a robot, because stupid SS-10K set him up to shut him down.

A favor I hope to return someday.

Someday soon.

CHAPTER 45

After school, I'm still scheming, still trying to come up with the Big Idea that'll simultaneously show the world how lame SS-10K is and how great E can be.

Since Dad is an idea guy, always cooking up twists and turns for his comic book plots, I decide to spitball a little with him. That's what writers call it when they bounce ideas off each other. No actual spitballs are involved.

But Dad's not in a brainstorming mood.

"I'm creatively blocked, Sammy," he says.

"What does that mean?"

"That I can't come up with any new ideas. Nobody wants *Hot and Sour Ninja Robots* anymore. Okay. Fine. So what *do* they want?"

I shrug. "I dunno. Trip would probably buy a manga about SS-10K rescuing another cat out of a tree."

"That's brilliant, Sammy. Brilliant!"

"Um, but he's the bad guy..."

"No. See, he's got muscles. That means he's the hero...."

So while Dad doodles, I slip outside and head over to Mom's workshop.

She's not in there working like I think she should be. Guess she's "creatively blocked," too.

I see what's left of my bro-bot, E, sitting on a workbench.

Okay, I know I'm probably not supposed to do this, but I need to talk to somebody I can trust. So I flick up the power switch on E's back. (If he starts singing the Notre Dame fight song again, I promise I'll power him down, fast.)

"Ah, good morning, Sammy. Was I in sleep mode?"

"Yeah."

He looks at his shoulders.

"Any idea what happened to my arms?"

Then he checks out his waist.

"Or my legs?"

"You had an accident."

"I did?"

"Yeah. You went kind of wild. I think SS-10K did something to scramble your brains. Somehow he short-circuited your central processing unit."

"Fascinating. I did feel a certain surge when the big fellow patted my back. I thought the warm feeling was just an overwhelming sense of robot pride. That SS-10K is a fine specimen of servo sophistication."

"He was messing with your motherboard! Infecting you with computer viruses."

"Well, the best cure for any virus is bed rest and plenty of fluids. I've had lots of sleep, and my hydraulic fluid levels seem fine—in my head and torso, anyway. So once I pull myself together, I will be ready to rock, as you say."

"That's good. But you're kind of grounded."

"I see. And how about you, Sammy? How are you feeling?"

"Not so good."

"Have you also been grounded?"

I shake my head. "No. This is worse than that."

Mom... DAD... MADDIE... NOTRE DAME... DR. INGALLS... SS-100... SCAM... CHEAT THE ARMY... MILLIONS OF DOLLARS... NEED AN IDEA... TRIP... HELMET... PEANUT BUTTER... BANANAS...

And finally, I unload. I tell E everything. About Dad and Mom and Dr. Ingalls. About SS-10K being a fake. About Dr. Ingalls trying to trick the US Army out of all sorts of money. About Eddie Ingalls not even having a brother. About how scared I was when they rushed Maddie back to the hospital. About how I promised her I'd make everything the way it used to be with E, only better.

I tell E *everything*.

He's a very good listener. (And, without legs, he can't walk away even if he *is* bored.)

We talk for like an hour.

And then Mom comes in.

With more bad news.

CHAPTER 46

How's it going, boys?" Mom asks as she enters her workshop and flicks on a few more lights.

Usually, Mom's robot workshop is the coolest place on earth. All sorts of mechanical creations buzz around the floor, helping Mom tinker with new projects.

Today? Not so much.

"I turned E on," I admit, figuring Mom will be ticked off about it. But she isn't. She seems distracted.

"Good afternoon, Professor Hayes," E peeps. "How are things at Notre Dame?"

"Not so good," she says with a sigh as she kind

of flops into her rolling work chair. "Unfortunately, Sammy had a little run-in with the law."

"Samuel? Surely you are mistaken."

"No, E," I say. "It's true. I was kind of snooping around Dr. Ingalls's house."

"Is this where you learned all those things we were talking about earlier?"

"Yeah."

"You should tell your mother what you discovered. Immediately."

I take a deep breath. I'm set to let it all out again, but Mom holds up her hand.

"Don't, Sammy. I can't hear any of what you think you may have heard outside that window at Dr. Ingalls's house. The lawyers at IRAT are claiming I sent you there to do 'intellectual espionage' for me."

"That's crazy!"

"They also say I was so desperate to save my own substitute student project that I made you go steal Dr. Ingalls's patented technology."

"That's not true," I say. "The spying was my idea. Totally."

"Sammy can be quite the creative thinker when he's motivated," adds E.

Mom gives us the thinnest smile. "Dean Schilpp says she admires all that I've done for the College of Engineering, but, well, it might be time for a change. Max Riley and a lot of the alumni agree. This weekend, after the big homecoming football game, they'll announce a new head for the ND robotics department. Dr. Ignatius Ingalls."

"Icky?" I shout. "No way. That bald buzzard's a big fat faker! He wants to cheat the government! And I can prove it!"

Mom holds up her hand again. "Don't, Sammy. Please? You'll only make things worse. As it is, I can still work at Notre Dame. I just have to stop all this." She gestures at her awesome workshop. "I'll also have to report to Dr. Ingalls."

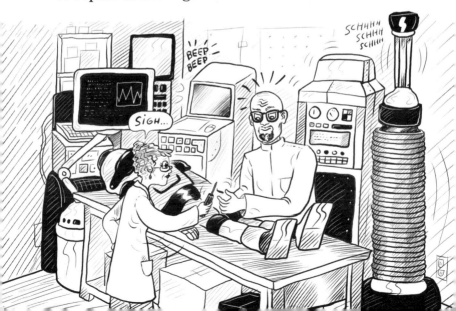

"No, Mom. You can't work for Dr. Ingalls. I know that he—"

"Sammy? I told you—we cannot have this conversation. Have you done your homework?"

"Not yet. I was kind of hoping E could help me out...."

"Fine. But don't stay out here too long. And be sure to shut off all the lights when you leave."

E and I exchange a look.

We're both feeling the same thing. Once I turn off those lights, they may never be turned back on.

And so we stay up for, like, six hours, and together, we cook up a plan. It's sort of based on Maddie's suggestion that I find a way to convince Mom to fix E *and* show the world that SS-10K is a fraud all at the same time.

It's a pretty good plan, if I do say so myself.

Like E said, I can be quite the creative thinker when I'm motivated.

CHAPTER 47

The next morning, the House of Robots isn't a very happy place.

Mr. Moppenshine tells all the other automatons that he overheard Mom tell Dad that "maybe we should shut down the workshop, move somewhere else, and start all over again."

"And they're not just gonna reboot us," says Hayseed. "I hear tell they're gonna give us the boot. So don't nobody stand too close to a can crusher."

"I don't want to be recycled!" screams Brittney 13, the hysterical, hyperventilating, mood-swinging teenager-bot Mom invented to test whether she could electronically reproduce human emotions. She could and she did. Brittney is a rolling emoticon.

I'M TOO YOUNG TO BE TURNED INTO A BICYCLE!

"Geoffrey?" I say to the butler-bot.

"Yes, Samuel?"

"Remember that 'keep calm and carry on' thing you told me?"

"Indeed."

"Tell it to the robots. Please. Nobody's getting

recycled or stripped for spare parts. But I am going to need each and every one of you in top physical condition."

"Very good, sir. May I inquire as to what task we will be performing for you?"

"Football."

"I beg your pardon?"

"Tell everybody to put on their game faces. I'll give you guys all the details once it's official. First, I have to go to Notre Dame."

"My goodness," says Geoffrey. "You're already attending college? My, oh my. Where *does* the time go? They grow up so fast...."

I kind of tiptoe through the kitchen, where Mom and Dad are drinking coffee and talking about moving.

"I can find a new college," says Mom.

"I can draw anywhere," says Dad.

"But all Maddie's doctors are here," says Mom.

"And her sterile room," adds Dad. "And all the hand-sanitizer pumps mounted to the walls."

"Keeping her care consistent won't be easy," says Mom.

"She really likes the doctors and staff at St. Joe's," says Dad.

And then they both see me. I almost made it out the door.

"Sammy?"

"Yes, Mom?"

"Why are you wearing a tie and your one good suit?"

"Because it's Dress Like a Grown-Up day at school."

"Well, I better run," I say.

"Be careful. Those are your Easter clothes."

"Don't worry. I'm not riding my bike today. I'm taking the bus."

Of course I don't tell them I don't mean the school bus.

I mean the bus to the Notre Dame campus!

CHAPTER 48

O kay, the real reason I'm all dressed up?

I'm taking the bus to the University of Notre Dame's College of Engineering building so I can visit my godmother, Dean Allison Schilpp. She once told me her "door was always open." She also said if I ever had any questions or concerns, I should come see her.

But she's still kind of surprised when I show up at her office.

HELLO, SAMMY. WHAT ARE YOU DOING HERE?

I HAVE SOME OF THOSE "QUESTIONS AND CONCERNS" YOU SAID I MIGHT HAVE SOMETIME.

"Come on in. Are you here because you're worried about your mother?"

"Mom? Ha! She's the best robotics professor in America. She'll find a new job in a nanosecond."

From the look on her face, I don't think that was the answer Dean Schilpp was expecting.

"But," I say, just the way E and I rehearsed it, "I am worried about *you*."

"Me?"

"Well, you and Notre Dame. What if Dr. Ignatius Ingalls isn't as good as he claims he is? What if he does something dumb to embarrass the university?"

"You mean like E and you have already done?"

I let that zinger roll right off me.

"No," I say smoothly, "I mean something way worse. What if his robots really aren't as good as Mom's?"

"But they are, Sammy."

"Then Dr. Ingalls shouldn't be afraid of a little friendly wager."

"Excuse me?"

"Mom's robots against his. You turn the annual mechatronic football game this Sunday into a huge event. If Mom's team wins, she keeps her job. If Dr.

Ingalls wins, she leaves town or does whatever you guys tell her to do, because everyone will see that you clearly made the right choice by going with Icky."

"Who?"

"Sorry. That's Dr. Ingalls's nickname. All of his friends call him that."

"Sammy, I can see the public relations value of your idea—"

"The robotic football game will be a sellout. Who knows? Maybe it'll be even bigger than the real home-coming game on Saturday."

"I sincerely doubt—"

"Call Dr. Ingalls," I suggest. "Tell him you've found something epic and spectacular that will, once and for all, prove SS-10K's superiority over anything Mom and her team could ever create."

Yep. I'm parroting Dr. Ingalls's words—the ones I heard while I was hiding in the bushes outside his window. I leave out the bit where he told his flunky that they needed to "publicly humiliate" my mother.

"I'm not sure Dr. Ingalls will agree to this, Sammy."

Good...I can tell she likes the idea.

"I guess there's only one way to find out," I say.

"Ask him. I have a feeling Dr. Ingalls is going to *loooove* a publicity stunt like this."

"Well, it *would* be a very exciting way to introduce Dr. Ingalls to the faculty and alumni," says Dean Schilpp.

All righty-o. She's definitely taking the bait.

She punches the speakerphone button and calls Dr. Ingalls to tell him "her" idea.

"What an excellent suggestion, Dean Schilpp," Icky says eagerly.

"This is just the sort of idea I was looking for to impress our very important friends down in Washington," says Dr. Ingalls.

"And if you should somehow happen to lose this football game, you agree that Dr. Hayes should stay on as head of my robotics department?"

"Of course. It's only fair. She doesn't stand a chance, but it's fair."

"Very well," says the dean. "I will instruct Dr. Hayes's emissary to make all the necessary arrangements."

Wow. I'm an emissary. It's amazing what you can be when you put on a suit and tie.

"Kickoff is three o'clock this Sunday," says Dean Schilpp.

"We'll be ready," says Dr. Ingalls.

Yes! It's on!

Now I just have to convince Mom to get E into shape for the big game, which is only three days away.

Because it'll be hard for him to play football without feet.

CHAPTER 49

I am definitely pumped. But before I head home to give Mom a much-needed pregame pep talk, I swing by the gym where the ND Mechatronic Football Club holds its practices.

Boxy contraptions that look like laser printers on wheels, miniature laundry carts, and high-tech catapults are whizzing and whirring around the shiny floor. Geeky-looking college kids in jeans and T-shirts thumb remote controls to put the robotic players through their paces. I look a little out of place in my suit.

The club's president, Joshua Chun, is one of Mom's graduate assistants.

"They want to fire Dr. Hayes?" he says after I explain the high stakes we'll be playing for this Sunday at the ND vs. IRAT Robot Bowl.

"Yup. And I know for a fact that Dr. Ingalls is a phony. So is his main player, SS-10K."

"The mechatronic dude who's always rescuing cats out of trees?"

"That was rigged," I say. "SS-10K is all show and no go. So are the empty-headed camo-coated battle-bots

Dr. Ingalls wants to sell to the army. We can beat these guys, Joshua."

"I don't know, Sammy. Our best players—RG3PO, the quarterback; and Airhead, the kicker—are pretty primitive. Yes, the quarterback has a GPS tracker, so he can tell where his receivers are and triangulate his toss trajectory, but that SS-10K is practically human. He'll be Peyton Manning, and we'll be Charlie Chun."

"Who's Charlie Chun?"

"My seven-year-old nephew. He plays quarterback for his Pee Wee Football team."

"Well, what if we drafted a bunch of players from Mom's workshop?"

"Seriously? She'd let E and Blitzen and the whole House of Robots crew play for ND?"

"Hey, they'll be playing for her job, too."

"Excellent." Joshua gets the intense look on his face that Mom always gets right before she starts spouting technical gobbledygook. "Okay, you're going to need to install a digital accelerometer on all the players. It'll sense if an upsetting event—knockdown, fall down, or tackle—has occurred. The sensor must then signal an LED light to turn red and simultaneously instruct the player's microprocessor to remove power from the drive system for two full seconds."

He goes on like that for maybe five minutes.

Fortunately, Joshua sends me home with a very thick Technical Appendix.

Unfortunately, there's no way for *me* to make the alterations we need to get the House of Robots team ready for the rules of Collegiate Mechatronic Football.

I can't do this thing without Mom's help.

When I get home, Trip is waiting for me in the driveway.

"Why weren't you in school today, Sammy?"

"I went to Notre Dame instead."

"Wow. You skipped, like, seven years and went straight to college? How'd you swing that? Did you take an IQ test or something?"

"I'm not *going* to college, Trip," I explain. "I just went to Notre Dame to make sure that E can still be Maddie's eyes and ears at Creekside Elementary."

"Oh. How'd you do that?"

"By talking my mom's boss into changing around the annual robotic football game so that it's between our robots and Dr. Ingalls's creepy creations. If the

House of Robots team wins, Mom keeps her job and E has his name cleared, once and for all."

"Be careful, Sammy," says Trip. "That SS-10K is a big cheat."

"I know. That's what I've been trying to tell you. But I thought you were in *loooove* with the stupid robot."

"I used to be. That's why I came over here this afternoon. To apologize. But first I stopped by the T-shirt shop."

Trip unzips his jacket so I can read his new slogan.

"What made you change your mind?" I ask.

"I went to that Robotics Club meeting. SS-10K taught us how to program our toy robots to do dirty tricks. Stuff like sending out signals to jam the other guy's remote control. 'You'll always be the best,' he said, 'if you make the other machine look its worst.'"

"That's exactly what he did to E!" I say. "He sabotaged him. Every time SS-10K touched E, the big

239

bully transmitted some kind of computer virus that made E go nutso."

"In that case," says Trip, "how exactly is this football game idea going to work?"

"We just have to make sure our bots never touch SS-10K."

"What? It's football, Sammy. Even the kind kindergartners play is called '*touch* football.' So how are you going to stop SS-10K from scrambling everybody's circuits again?"

"I'm not sure," I admit. "I'm kind of hoping Mom can come up with some sort of special anti-electronic padding or something. Maybe a force field."

"Seriously?"

"The game's not till Sunday."

"So she has two days to invent a force field generator?"

"Or the padding."

"Right."

Now we're both just nodding and not saying anything.

Oh boy.

I need Mom's help.

Big-time!

Trip wishes me luck as he heads home and I head into Mom's workshop.

E is slumped on the worktable. He has one arm. No legs. He also looks like he's in sleep mode. Mom is tapping the "end call" icon on her smartphone.

"Sammy?" says Mom, swiveling around in her chair. "Did you go to Notre Dame today instead of going to school?"

"Yes, Mom," I say bravely. "I most certainly did."

"And did you talk Dean Schilpp into changing the terms of her robotic football game to a ridiculous contest between my robots and Dr. Ingalls's?"

This time, I stiffen my spine a little. "Yes, Mom. I most certainly did. But I wouldn't call it 'ridiculous.'"

"I would. What on earth were you thinking, Samuel

Hayes-Rodriguez?"

Okay, have you ever seen the movies *Rocky* or *Rudy*? If so, please start humming the heroic sound track in your head. I know I am.

"What was I thinking?" I say, clasping my hands

behind my back and pacing back and forth in front of Mom, the way I've seen football coaches do when they give the big speech at halftime that fires up their team. "I was thinking that it's time to fight for what's right."

"What?"

"Tell me, Mom, is it right that Maddie can't go to

school because of SS-10K?"

"Maddie can't go to school because of what E did."

I stop pacing. Look my mother square in the eye. "You mean what E did after SS-10K messed him up!"

"Sammy, you keep saying that, but…"

"It's true," says E, his head snapping up.

"I thought I powered you down," says Mom.

"Actually, Professor Hayes, you put me in sleep mode. But what Sammy is saying is too important for me to snooze through. He is correct. SS-10K infected my circuits with a rogue virus."

Mom shakes her head. "Impossible."

"Impossible?" I say. "Impossible? Aren't you the one who always tells me that with science, anything is possible? That if I can dream it, I can do it?"

"Well, yes, but…"

"Well, some scientists have bad dreams, Mom. They dream up horrible, evil stuff. And they'll keep on dreaming it up until someone comes along to stop them. We need to fight for what's right!"

Yep, this time, it's *me* giving Mom the lecture.

And from the look on her face, I can tell it's working!

CHAPTER 52

Put me in, Coach!" says E.

"B-b-but," Mom stammers.

SOMEONE NEEDS TO STOP DR. IGNATIUS INGALLS AND ALL HIS EVIL SCHEMES. SOMEONE IN SHOULDER PADS AND A HELMET. SOMEONE I LIKE TO CALL **E** BECAUSE HE IS SO EXCEPTIONALLY EXCELLENT.

"What've we got to lose?" I say.

"Nothing, I guess," says Mom.

"And if we win this game, you keep your job, E's slate is wiped clean, and, best of all, Dr. Icky Ingalls goes away while Maddie goes back to the third grade. You just have to protect E from SS-10K's electronic shenanigans."

Mom turns to E. "How exactly does this other robot interfere with your operational integrity?"

Good. She's talking techno mumbo jumbo. She's in it to win it!

E explains how he goes whackaloon whenever SS-10K touches him. I tell Mom how I saw the same thing happen with a toy robot.

"So, somehow we have to block SS-10K's electronic invasion of your circuitry," Mom mumbles, as her pen hovers over a sketchpad. "We need to shield your sensors...."

"You have two days, Mom," I say, cheering her (and her brain) on. "Sure, you would've had a lot more time if you had listened to me sooner. But that's water under the bridge. Nothing we can do about your bad decision now. So, Dr. Elizabeth Hayes, best robotics brain in the whole entire universe, I really only have one question." I wait for a second. *"Can you do this thing?"*

She jumps out of her chair. "Yes, I can!"

"Good," I say. "Now get back to work!"

**CHAPTER
53**

The next day, while Mom tinkers with E, Trip and I help her assistant Joshua Chun install digital tackle-sensor gizmos on all our other players.

"The games are usually eight on eight," says Joshua as he continues going over the rules of Collegiate Mechatronic Football. "But the folks at IRAT want to keep this simpler. Five on five."

"Okay," I say.

"But," says Trip, "what if E isn't ready in time?"

"He will be."

"But what if he isn't, Sammy? The game's tomorrow. At three."

"And," adds Joshua, "Dr. Hayes told me she still hasn't found a way to effectively block SS-10K's electronic interference. And even if she did, she wouldn't have time to install it on any of our other robots."

"Don't worry," I say. "All we need is for E to be able to play defense. Come on. We need to practice with the players who aren't on the disabled list."

Since E isn't cleared to play, we put Hayseed into the quarterback position. Blitzen and Geoffrey the

butler will be his linemen. I want Drone Malone to be our primary receiver, but Joshua tells me that "flying" robots are against the rules.

"All bots must be in contact with the gym floor at all times."

"Unless they get tackled," says Trip. "Right?"

"Actually," I say, "they're even more 'in contact with the floor' when that happens."

So we put Mr. Moppenshine in as wide receiver. The guy's got three arms and three legs. Our running back is McFetch.

He can clamp the ball between his jaws, and once he does, nobody is tearing it out of his mouth. He's very doggish that way. He's also a very speedy and tricky runner. I once chased him around and around the couch for like an hour without catching him.

"All right, huddle up," says Hayseed, kneeling on the lawn and scratching out a play in the dirt. "We're gonna run us the famous Breadbasket Blubber Belly play."

"I beg your pardon?" says Geoffrey.

"It's a classic," says Hayseed. "Right up there with the Statue of Liberty and Flea Flicker and them other trick plays. I fake a handoff to McFetch. Blitzen? You and butler-boy pretend like you're blockin' for the dog. Meanwhile, Mr. Moppenshine runs downfield and starts in to twirling his dust mop and vacuum cleaner and shoutin', 'Yoo-hoo, throw me the ball.'

"While the other team is distracted," Hayseed continues, "I hide the football under the bib of my overalls and pretend like I just had me a big lunch. I pat my stomach and say, 'Shoo-wee, I ate so much, I gotta go lie down.' Then I just waddle down the field and score a touchdown."

"Seriously?" I say.

"Heck yeah, Coach. Works all the time."

"But robots don't eat lunch. They don't eat food at all."

"Well, I'm countin' on the other team not knowin' that."

"They're robots, too."

"Oh. Right. Okay. I got me another trick play. Call it the Hook and Ladder. We're gonna need us a hook and a ladder...."

I look over to Mom's workshop and say a silent prayer.

We really, really, *really* need E.

CHAPTER 54

Sunday comes sooner than I want it to.

Mom's still in her workshop, tinkering away on E.

"I think I've finally figured out a way to shield E from SS-10K," she says.

"And," says Dad, who's in there helping, "I drew up the design!"

"Your family is so awesome, Sammy," says Trip.

"Yeah," I say. "I know."

"I mean, everybody works together. Like peanut butter and bananas."

Even Maddie is in the workshop (well, virtually) as our head cheerleader.

"E, did you get all those plays I downloaded to your hard drive?" Maddie asks from an iPad propped on the workbench.

"I certainly did," says E, sounding super chipper again.

"You guys?" I say. "It's two thirty! Kickoff is in thirty minutes!"

"Just need a little more time to reinforce these shields," says Mom. "You go on, Sammy. Start the game without E."

"We'll join you as soon as we can," adds Dad.

Trip and I take off for Notre Dame with Joshua, who's been waiting in the driveway for us with his motor running.

"Where's your mom and E?" he asks.

"Still suiting up for the game," I say. "Let's roll!"

Tires squealing, we take off. Fortunately, the gym at the Stepan Center is only a five-minute drive from our house.

"The game will be sixty minutes long," Joshua explains from behind the wheel. "Four fifteen-minute quarters. There's a robot band at halftime. They mostly play techno."

"Will Max Riley and all the other bigwigs be there?"
I ask.

"Front row. Right behind the IRAT bench."

All righty-o. I guess we know which team Mr. Riley
is rooting for.

CHAPTER 55

At exactly three PM, the game starts—without our star player.

Mr. Moppenshine uses all three of his dust-mop legs to kick off.

SS-10K catches the ball at the goal line.

"Flying V formation!" he calls out.

The four other bots on the IRAT team *ZHISH-WHIRR-ZHISH* into an angled-wedge configuration in front of SS-10K. They lock arms, shift into forward drive, and proceed to bulldoze their way up the floor like a snowplow on the front end of a locomotive.

They quickly shove Geoffrey the butler out of their way. Blitzen can't ram through their ranks, even

though he plays bumper cars like crazy with them. McFetch starts yapping at the ankles of the robot at the tip of the wedge. The big galoot reaches down and pats the robo-pooch on his head. The whole crowd packed into the gym goes, "Awwww," and several hundred smartphones capture another cute-puppy video clip.

But when the robot is done petting McFetch, the mechanical dog spins around like a crazy windup toy. The kind with swirling swivel wheels. McFetch isn't foaming at the mouth like mad dogs usually do, but his snout is definitely sparking.

Yep. Team IRAT just short-circuited another one of Mom's creations.

SS-10K rumbles untouched all the way to the goal line. Indiana Robotics and Automaton Tech score the first points of the Robot Bowl.

"Put me in, Coach!" shrieks Brittney 13, the robot bursting with all the feelings of a teenage girl. Right now, I think she's running her "I hate all of you" emotional program, because I have never seen her look so mad. All her LEDs are blinking red.

I send her in to replace McFetch, who's definitely going on the twenty-one-day disabled list (maybe for the rest of his life).

Trip puts our wounded canine warrior in a doggy carrier. It bounces around like a self-propelled basketball.

The poor guy's circuits have been deep-fried to a crackly crunch.

"Referee?" drones SS-10K. He's pointing at Brittney 13. "Her red LEDs are blinking!"

According to the rule book, those sensors we had to install on all our bots makes them blink red if they've been officially tackled. When that happens, they have to remain "immobile" for two seconds. But even though Brittney hasn't even had a chance to play, she's so mad that her red LEDs started throbbing. In her cheeks, her ears, and her eyeballs.

The referee blows a whistle. "According to your sensors, you've been tackled, like, five hundred times. We're putting your motor drive on lockdown. You're officially out of the game!"

"You heard the referee!" shouts Dr. Ingalls. "Pull her off the field."

Blitzen does the honors. He sort of shoves Brittney to the sidelines.

"You'll be sorry you did that, Icky!" Brittney screams. "Super sorry!" Then she sits down on the bench and pouts.

We're down to four fully functioning players.

Drone Malone hovers down the bench to beep at me.

"I'm sorry," I tell him. "I can't put you in the game. The rules say no flying."

"Don't worry, Coach," says Blitzen. "Even with just four players, we can take these guys."

"We'll mop the floor with them," says (you guessed it) Mr. Moppenshine.

"Indubitably!" adds Geoffrey.

I just nod.

And stare at the door.

And pray that E shows up.

Soon!

**CHAPTER
56**

With two minutes left in the second quarter, the score is Indiana Robotics and Automaton Tech 49, Notre Dame Robotics Club 00.

IRAT calls a time-out. They've scored so many points, they all need a quick lube job.

To make matters worse, Penelope Pettigrew, in a cheesy cheerleader costume she probably wore for Halloween, is over with Eddie Ingalls and all the very important alumni eager to fire Mom.

"And," says Mr. Riley, the mega-donor to the College of Engineering, "three cheers for our new department head, Dr. Ignatius Ingalls!"

There's a lot of "hip-hip-hooraying" from the IRAT bleachers.

This isn't a football game.

This is, basically, Mom's professional funeral.

"Not to worry," says Geoffrey, sliding over to me and Trip. "Keep a stiff upper lip, lads."

"Easy for you to say," mumbles Trip. "You're made out of metal. Both your lips are stiff!"

"Easy, kid," says Blitzen. "We're a team. A team doesn't turn on itself, even when the chips are down. Remember my motto: Get knocked down seven times, stand up eight."

"But you've been knocked down fifteen times! At least!"

"And I'm still getting up. Because you give one hundred percent in the first half of the game, and if that isn't enough, in the second half you give what's left."

I'm hoping for a miracle. Because E may never show up. Maybe he was damaged beyond repair. Maybe Mom decided to call it quits. Maybe I was nuts to think we could ever pull this thing off and beat Dr. Ingalls at his own game.

The ref blows his whistle, and our four remaining robots hobble onto the field.

After the snap, SS-10K drops back to pass, probably another long bomb.

But Blitzen blitzes. He zooms past all the IRAT blockers and slams into SS-10K's foot, tripping him up enough to force a fumble. In the confusion, Blitzen scoops up the ball and races down the sideline, his tank treads rolling so fast, he's smoking up the floor.

I'm jumping up and down for joy. I turn to "woo-hoo" with Trip.

And over his shoulder, I see Dr. Ingalls tap a shiny shamrock lapel pin.

Out on the field, Blitzen is in the clear. There's not a tackler in sight. He's at the twenty. The fifteen.

He's going to score!

No.

He's not.

He stops.

Right on the five-yard line.

He pivots around. Does a 180.

"Turn back around!" I holler.

But Blitzen zips upfield. In the wrong direction.

He runs ninety yards in nine seconds. When he gets near the goal line at the opposite end of the field, he tosses the ball to SS-10K, who is waiting patiently at the one-yard line.

SS-10K slips across the goal line.

Thanks to Blitzen, IRAT scores again.

After the extra kick, I hear a whistle, a boat horn, and a whole bunch of techno.

It's halftime.

The score?

Indiana Robotics and Automaton Tech 56, Notre Dame Robotics Club 00.

CHAPTER 57

The marching robot band takes the field.

They're pretty good. They even do a Shamrock formation. I sort of wish some of the band members could play on my football team, because I've pretty much run out of robots.

Blitzen's circuits have been blitzed and blotched and *KA-BLOOIED*.

Mad Dog McFetch is still thrashing around in his pet carrier.

Brittney 13 is still flashing red with anger, rage, and resentment.

The only players we have left are Hayseed, Geoffrey, Mr. Moppenshine, and the grounded Drone Malone.

"We need to go home and see why it's taking so long to fix E," I say to Joshua. "They're not answering their phones."

"What about the game?" he asks.

"Trip can coach what's left of our team until we get back."

"Can I have Hayseed try that blubber belly breadbasket ball-hiding thingie?" Trip asks.

"Try anything you want, Trip. We'll be back as soon as we can. And, hopefully, E will be with us!"

Joshua and I race toward the door, which means we have to run past the IRAT cheering section.

"Where you going, Sammy?" sneers Eddie Ingalls.

"Are you forfeiting the game?" asks Dean Schilpp.

"None of us would blame you if you quit, kid," adds Max Riley.

"We're not quitting," I shout as I keep running. "We're just getting warmed up!"

We hop into Joshua's car and blast off for home.

It's a wild ride, but it gives me a few minutes to think.

About Maddie.

She's always loved football, especially Notre Dame

football. But she's never been able to go to an actual game.

With E, she could do the next best thing. He could sit in the stands for her. Be her eyes and ears in the stadium, just like he does in the classroom. But there's only one way to make that happen.

We have to win the Robot Bowl.

As we whip out of Notre Dame, I catch a glimpse of Touchdown Jesus.

I think he's cheering for us.

That makes me smile.

When it comes to cheerleaders, I'll take Jesus over Penelope Pettigrew any day of the week—and twice on Sunday!

CHAPTER 58

I burst into Mom's workshop.

Right away, I see a huge problem: Nobody's *working*.

"You guys?" I say. "What's going on?"

Mom and Dad both sigh.

"We're done," says Mom.

"With E? Great. Because..."

"No, Sammy," says Dad. "Your mother means we're finished here in South Bend."

"This football game was a clever idea," says Mom, "but Dr. Ingalls's robots are just better than mine."

"And I can't draw anymore," adds Dad. "I'm like an empty ink bottle. I'm all out."

I can't believe this.

"Seriously?" I say. "You're quitting? Both of you? You're just giving up?"

Mom and Dad both nod, looking really tired. "Yeah," they say. "We are."

I gape at them, but can't think of anything to say. Like Dad, I'm all out…of pep talks.

But then we hear a voice.

"Welcome to my world," says Maddie. She's talking to us from an iPad on Mom's desk.

"What?" says Mom.

"Do you know how many times I've wanted to call it quits? To give up? Every time I go to the hospital! But if I quit, that means I'm giving up hope, too. And without hope, what do I have left? A very nice, very clean room and some equally nice, clean robots. But what if there's a chance I can one day beat this disease? What if some brainy scientist out there finds a cure? What if the day they find that cure, I'm not around because I decided to call it quits when the going got tough? Well, as somebody once said, 'When the going gets tough, the tough get going!'"

I nod. "Our gym teacher says that all the time."

"Because he's right. So, Mom?"

"Yes, dear?"

"Pick up that screwdriver. Make your final adjustments. Dad? Lend her a hand. E's going to Notre Dame, right now, to play some robotic football. Because the only way to win this game is to be in it! Life isn't a spectator sport!"

"Maddie's right, you guys!" I say.

"We know!" says Dad.

"We taught her that!" adds Mom.

And, in a flash, they finish fixing E!

E and I will hurry back to the game in Joshua's car. Mom and Dad will follow behind us in the van. Maddie will watch the rest of the game from her room, and if anything bad happens while we're all away from home, she'll call Dylan and Dave at the hospital. She has their phone number. It's 9-1-1.

When I get back to the Stepan Center, the third quarter is just under way.

And SS-10K has already rung up another fourteen points.

CHAPTER 59

The only player Trip has left is Hayseed, and he's basically playing Keep Away.

SHOOWEE! I'M AS SCARED AS A LONG-TAILED CAT IN A ROOM FULL OF ROCKING CHAIRS.

The score is Indiana Robotics and Automaton Tech 70, Notre Dame Robotics Club 00.

"Excellent," says E as he hustles into the gym. "We only need to score ten touchdowns and ten extra points!"

Trip sees us coming and calls a time-out. The referee blows his whistle.

There are ten minutes remaining in the third quarter; twenty-five minutes left in the whole game.

"We need to score a touchdown every two and a half minutes," says E, who always does math much faster than me.

Mom and Dad take seats in the bleachers—right next to Dean Schilpp. That means they're pretty close to all those big-deal alumni guys and right behind the IRAT bench.

"I'm so sorry your career has to end this way, Liz," says Dean Schilpp.

"Hey, it's not over till it's over," says Mom. "Isn't that right, Dr. Ingalls?"

"Well, Lizzie," says Dr. Ingalls, sort of smugly, "I believe overcoming a lead this large will prove mathematically impossible for your team."

"Maybe. But as my son, Sammy, recently reminded me, with science, anything is possible."

Wow.

Mom is quoting me. I think that's a first.

I turn to E and say, "Go in there and fight, fight, fight!"

"Actually," says E, "I prefer to start with a handshake."

And he heads out to say hello to SS-10K.

"Wait!" I run after him. "Don't let him touch you! If SS-10K scrambles your circuits again, we lose our last chance!"

E shoots me a wink and flashes me his new, extremely cool-looking football gloves.

"Mom didn't want my hands getting cold," he whispers. "She also applied a very thin rubberized coating over my entire body. I'm sealed up tighter than a microwavable shrink-wrapped sandwich."

"You have lost the game, Eggbeater," says SS-10K when the two bots meet at midfield.

"Really?" says E. "Sammy tells me there are still twenty-five minutes left to play."

"Ample time for you to demonstrate how inferior your operating system truly is."

E extends his hand and says, "May the best bot win."

"You mean me? Of course I will prove triumphant, Eggbreath."

"Sorry. You are incorrect. My name is E."

E takes SS-10K's hand and shakes it hard. A look of confusion lights up the evil eyes behind the big bot's tinted visor.

"What's the matter?" E asks with a smile. "Having trouble accessing my hard drive? Fascinating. I have no problem accessing yours."

"Let's play ball!" shouts the referee, who, I think, isn't used to robot trash talk.

Since the IRAT team just scored, they have to kick off to E and Hayseed.

SS-10K boots the ball.

E catches it.

And then he takes off.

Who knew he could run so fast?

"In addition to my rubberized shell, Mom also gave me a turbo boost!" he hollers as he zips past me like a rocket.

Our cheering section leaps to its feet.

It's only Mom, Dad, and a couple of her grad students, but they're very loud and happy.

"Woo-hoo!" they all shout.

E made it to the end zone! He scored our first points of the game!

After doing a quick end zone dance, E tosses the ball to the referee.

"We need to move speedily," he tells the official. "We have a lot of ground to make up. I need to score a touchdown every two point five minutes."

Now it's our turn to kick off. When one of the IRAT players catches E's line-drive bullet of a ball, his chest gets dented. And he topples backward. On IRAT'S own three-yard line.

On the very next play, E slams into SS-10K as he's dropping back to pass.

The IRAT robot's red tackle lights blink. His motor cuts out.

"Safety!" shouts the referee, because the dummy froze in his own end zone.

That means we get another two points, plus IRAT has to kick off to us again.

The rest of the third quarter goes our way.

Every time E kicks off, another IRAT player bites the dust with a fresh dent dinged into his chest. Dr. Ingalls keeps sending in replacements, but they keep going down. It's almost like they're bowling pins.

Add in a few more boosts of E's new turbo speed, and all of a sudden the game is wide open.

At the end of the third quarter, the scoreboard looks a lot better: Indiana Robotics and Automaton Tech 70, Notre Dame Robotics Club 39.

So, in the fourth quarter, the IRAT team decides it's time to start playing even dirtier.

CHAPTER 60

The next time E kicks off, SS-10K catches the ball and hovers maybe ten feet off the ground as he floats downfield.

"That's against the rules!" I shout.

Joshua flips through his official rule book while E springs up to grab SS-10K's feet as he streaks overhead. With a little help from Hayseed, E is able to tackle (okay, drag) SS-10K down to the ground—ten yards away from the goal line.

I turn to Joshua. "Tell the ref what you told me."

"All bots must be in contact with the gym floor at all times," he reads from the rule book.

"Really?" scoffs Dr. Ingalls. "That is such a restrictive rule. How can we ever hope to make giant technological leaps forward if we are forever hemmed in by such ridiculous regulations?"

"He's right," says Max Riley. "Rewrite the rule book. Let the bots fly if they can."

Dean Schilpp turns to Mom. "Dr. Hayes? Your opinion on the flying-robot rule?"

Mom shrugs. "Fish got to swim, bots got to fly."

Dean Schilpp stands up and addresses the crowd. "Ladies and gentlemen, in the fourth and final quarter of the Robot Bowl, flying and/or hovering *will* be allowed."

The whole crowd "oohs" and "aahs."

I look to Mom. I'm nervous. She isn't. In fact, she's smiling. Then she nods at Drone Malone.

Of course! I turn to my bench. "Malone? You're in the game!"

The drone beeps and bloops excitedly at me. He is a bot of few words.

Meanwhile, E is adjusting something on his ankle.

"Are you okay?" I ask, worried that he sprained his leg gear leaping up like he did to snare SS-10K in midair.

"Fine and dandy. Especially since I now understand why Mom took so long making my repairs."

"Huh?"

"She wanted to install a pair of what she called 'maglev hover boots.' I told her we were running late. She said, 'Well, with these, you'll be running on air if Dr. Ingalls tries to rewrite the rules like he always does.' It made absolutely no sense at the time."

I'm grinning like crazy. "Well, it sure does now!"

No wonder Mom took so much time fixing E. She was souping him up! Giving him all sorts of new features.

My whole game plan in the fourth quarter is what you might call an air attack, because we have two flying players. And one of them can cruise at an altitude of five thousand feet (though not in this gym).

With Hayseed hiking the ball, E playing quarterback, and Drone Malone catching everything that

comes his way, we're tossing touchdowns every time we snap the ball.

And when IRAT has the pigskin, Drone Malone and E are both blocking their aerial assault with something I like to call the iron-dome defense.

CHAPTER
61

There's only one minute left on the clock.

And we're still four points behind!

But *we* have the ball.

SS-10K gets desperate and tries pulling some of his old tricks.

"I will warp your random access memory!" he screams, charging across the line of scrimmage on the next play like Frankenstein's monster. "I will destroy your control functions as I did prior to the last time you visited Notre Dame!"

The whole crowd gasps.

Yep. The big bully is pretty loud, and he just basically made a public confession.

Dean Schilpp turns to Mom. "SS-10K sabotaged E? What Sammy said was true!"

I don't let it go to my head. Because now we only have fifty-five seconds left to win this game, and SS-10K is out there going ballistic, chasing after E, who bobs and weaves and jukes and jives and scores another touchdown!

We're winning!

And there are only forty-five seconds left on the clock.

"Put me in, Coach." It's Blitzen. "I'm feeling much better."

"I'm not sure," I say.

"It was a temporary mental meltdown," says Blitzen. "A few extra volts surging through my brain. I shook it off. I'm good to go."

It's TIME TO mow THEiR LAWN, COACH!

I let Blitzen take the field with E, Drone Malone, and Hayseed.

We kick off.

The ball hits SS-10K in the chest and he *ZHOOSH-CHUG-ZHOOSHES* up the field with it, right toward Blitzen.

And Blitzen just sits there. Revving his wheels. Churning up a cloud of smoke.

Uh-oh. Maybe I shouldn't have put him in. I'm

thinking we're going to lose the game in the final minute, when, all of a sudden, Blitzen blasts off!

I think that extra electricity he ate when they fizzled his circuits has totally recharged his batteries. He barrels down the field like a tank and slams squarely into SS-10K. The ball pops free. Hayseed falls on the fumble.

"My knees!" drones SS-10K loudly. "They have been permanently damaged. Dr. Ingalls, I warned you against using these cheap, junky parts!"

A man in a military uniform with lots of stripes and medals points at Dr. Ingalls.

"Your robots are useless, Professor Ingalls!" says the guy, who might be an army general. "We will be canceling our order with you immediately!"

Dr. Ingalls spits and sputters, but there's nothing he can say.

Now there are only forty seconds left on the clock.

Smiling, I finally relax. Because we have the ball *and* the lead.

But forty seconds is still plenty of time for some people to do a lot of damage.

People like Eddie Ingalls and Penelope Pettigrew!

CHAPTER
62

With only forty seconds left on the clock and the injured SS-10K out of the game, E elects to be a good sport and not run up the score.

So, on the next play he decides to "take a knee."

That's what they call it when you don't actually run a play. You just take the ball and, once the clock starts up, you basically tackle yourself by kneeling down.

Which makes him an easy target for two of SS-10K's biggest fans.

Suddenly, Eddie Ingalls and Penelope Pettigrew come charging at E with a bright orange bucket of Gatorade. They're too fast for even him to move away!

"You're going down, Eggbreath!" screams Penelope.

"This is for my twin sister, Betty!" shouts Eddie.

If Eddie and Penelope can short-circuit E before he uses the next play to take another knee, Dr. Icky Ingalls might be able to rally his other robots, steal the ball back, and have one last chance to score!

They swing back the sloshing bucket. Green liquid is splashing up and dribbling over the lip.

They aim for E's head.

I can't look!

Suddenly, someone screams, "No you don't, gal-dern it!"

I peek open an eye.

It's Hayseed! He dives between E and the bucket to take the hit.

The poor bot gets drenched. Circuits sizzle. Sparks sputter. Hayseed's limbs start quivering like they're loaded with Mexican jumping beans.

"Hasta la vista, y'all," says Hayseed. And he conks out.

E stands up.

And it's Maddie's voice that comes out of his mouth. "Penelope Pettigrew, you should be ashamed of yourself. What did Ms. Tracey teach us about playing fair?"

"That it's a stupid thing to do?" says Eddie.

"No," says Maddie through E. "Winners never cheat and cheaters never win. You're also supposed to say you're sorry when you hurt somebody."

"Ha!" sneers Penelope. "That thing on the floor is a robot. It's not a 'somebody.'"

"You are wrong, Miss Pettigrew," says E, with his own voice. "He *is* somebody. He is my friend."

E picks Hayseed up. Tucks him under his arm.

"Referee? Kindly restart the clock. We still have time to score a few more points."

Once the ref clears Eddie and Penelope off the floor (and a janitor mops up the Gatorade puddle), Dean Schilpp gives the signal to restart the game clock.

She also gives Eddie Ingalls and his dad a very nasty look.

I don't think she's so crazy about the idea of Professor Icky heading up her robotics department anymore.

Meanwhile, with Blitzen blocking everything in his path, E puts the football into Hayseed's limp hands and carries his broken friend across the goal line.

Yep. The final points of the Robot Bowl are officially scored by our conked-out gardener.

ND wins the game!

Mom keeps her job!

And, best of all, Maddie's going back to school with E!

Then, impossible as it may seem, things get even better.

CHAPTER 63

E xcuse me, ladies and gentlemen," E says to his audience. "It's time for the postgame show."

He gently lowers Hayseed to the floor.

"Kindly turn your attention to the video monitors arrayed around the room."

Turns out, when the two bots shook hands, E downloaded all sorts of digital data that SS-10K recorded on his hard drive over the past few weeks through his eyeball cams.

Now the whole world—well, everybody in the Stepan Center, including Mom's boss and all those very important alumni—sees what I always suspected. SS-10K is a big phony.

First we're treated to close-ups of all the framed photos of Eddie at Dr. Ingalls's house.

God Bless Our One
and Only Child

"There is no twin?" says Max Riley. "The whole 'substitute student' thing was a sham and a charade?"

Dr. Ingalls doesn't say anything.

Next, E projects raw footage of SS-10K's heroic exploits. Most of it, however, is "before" stuff. Like, before the robot rescues the cat out of the tree, we see a guy in an IRAT lab coat putting the cat into the tree and duct-taping its paws to the branches.

We also see how E was framed at the zoo and the pet store and even the Studebaker Museum.

"Would you like to see more?" asks E. "I have hours of material."

"No, thank you," says Dean Schilpp. "We've seen enough. Dr. Ingalls? The job is no longer available."

"We're sticking with Dr. Elizabeth Hayes," adds Max Riley.

"And we're promoting her!" says Dean Schilpp.

"Ha!" fumes Dr. Ingalls. "You haven't heard the last of me or my machines."

"Oh yes, we have," says this huge, hulking guy with a buzz cut and a neck the size of a tree stump. He's with six of his huge stump-necked buddies. They're the Notre Dame football players who corralled E when he went wild in front of Touchdown Jesus at the stadium.

"Let's go, Icky," says one of the players. "The sooner you're off campus, the sooner E can teach us his awesome plays."

"I want a pair of those rocket boots, too, Dr. Hayes," says another.

They firmly escort Dr. Ingalls and Eddie out of the gym.

When they're finally out the door, Dean Schilpp turns to Mom.

"Liz, I'm sorry. I was wrong. Will you accept a promotion to Assistant Dean?"

"It all depends," says Mom.

"What do you want? A bigger office? Extra staff? More research funds?"

"That'd be nice. But what I'd really like is for you to make one very important phone call."

"To the Nobel Prize people?"

"No, Ali. Just call Creekside Elementary. Tell them E is safe to go back into Maddie's third-grade classroom."

"Done!"

"Hey, you guys!" Dad says to me and Trip. "Check this out. I just had a wild idea for a new graphic novel. What do you two think?"

THE ROBO-BALL ALL-STARS SAVE THE GALAXY!

"I love it, Mr. Rodriguez," says Trip.

"Me too, Dad!"

"Excellent work, sir," says E, who's come over to admire the drawing.

And guess what?

Later that day, when Dad sends his Robo-Ball sketch to his publisher, they love it, too. He's officially working again!

CHAPTER 64

On Monday morning I'm so excited, I'm up and out of bed before Buzz, the floating alarm-clock-bot, zips in to blast my eardrums.

Maddie's going back to school today! Well, E is going back for her.

It's a beautiful fall morning, so Trip, E, and I ride our bikes.

We don't take any bizarro detours, either.

When we arrive at school, Mrs. Reyes, the principal, shakes E's hand.

"So glad to have you and Maddie back."

"Thank you, Mrs. Reyes!" says Maddie through E. "And now that all this craziness is over, I hope you and Mom and Dad can get back to gigging with your band."

I close my eyes. I wish Maddie hadn't said that.

They don't call themselves the Almost Pretty Bad band for nothing. They're Not Very Good. Actually, they Pretty Much Stink.

Principal Reyes informs us that "neither Eddie Ingalls nor his twin brother, Freddy Teddy Neddy," will be coming back to Creekside Elementary.

"They've moved to Illinois so his father can teach at *their* robot and automaton technical school."

Makes sense. Indiana, Illinois. They both start with the same letter. Dr. Ingalls can still use all his leftover IRAT lab coats. And if Illinois doesn't work out, he can move to Iowa.

On our way to Mrs. Kunkel's classroom, we bump into Jacob Gorski.

"Congratulations," he says.

"You watched the game?"

Jacob nods. "So did the rest of the Robotics Club. Then we took a vote. It was unanimous. We want E to be our new president."

"But that's your job," says Trip.

"Nah. I was no good at it. I even let that seriously evil SS-10K ruin my brand-new EV3RSTORM."

"Let me take it home someday after school," I say. "My mom will fix it."

Jacob's eyes widen. "Do you think she can?"

"Are you kidding?" says Trip. "Sammy's mom can fix anything, except maybe a peanut-butter-and-banana sandwich."

E smiles and says (in his own voice), "Dr. Hayes can work wonders, Jacob. When it comes to bringing robots back to their full potential, she is quite skilled and talented. Just like her son."

Okay. The big guy's making me blush a little.

As for Penelope Pettigrew, Ms. Tracey has given her a new job. She's in charge of making sure that E has the best seat in the third-grade classroom and always has his battery charger plugged in. Otherwise, she'll be sent down to kindergarten for a few months to relearn her manners.

And me?

Well, every day right around three, when the final bell rings, Maddie signs off, and E becomes E again.

Then he and I just sort of hang out, the way brothers do.

And, sometimes, like brothers everywhere, we even talk about football.

CHAPTER 1

Hi, I'm Sammy Hayes-Rodriguez. Maybe you've heard of me? I'm the kid everybody's making fun of because my mother made me bring a robot to school with me—the dumbest, most embarrassing thing to ever happen to any kid in the whole history of school. (I'm talking about going back to the Pilgrims and Mayflower Elementary.)

I need to tell you a wild and crazy story about this robot that—I kid you not—thinks it's my brother.

And guess where the dumb-bot got that goofy idea?

From my mother!

Hi, I'm SAMMY'S FRIEND TRIP. I'M NOT EVEN IN THIS CHAPTER, BUT HERE I AM ANYWAY.

Oh, guess what? My father is in on this idiotic robot business, too. He even called Mom's lame-o idea "brilliant."

Good thing Maddie is still on my side.

Maddie's absolutely the best little sister anybody could ever have. Aren't her blue eyes incredible? Oh, right. *Duh.* That drawing is in black-and-white. Well, trust me—her eyes are bluer than that Blizzard

Blue crayon in the jumbo sixty-four-color box.

Anyway, Maddie and I talked about Mom's latest screwy scheme over breakfast, which, of course, was served by one of Mom's many wacky inventions: the Breakfastinator.

MADDIE

Punch the button for Cap'n Crunch and cereal tumbles into a bowl, which slides down to the banana slicer, shuffles off to the milk squirter, scoots over to the sugar sprinkler, and zips down to the dispenser window.

THE BREAKFASTINATOR!

Want some OJ with your cereal? Bop the orange button.

But—and this is super important—do NOT push the orange juice and Cap'n Crunch buttons at the same time. Trust me. It's even worse if you push Cap'n Crunch and scrambled eggs.

Maddie and I always have breakfast together before I head off to school. The two of us talk about everything, even though Maddie's two years younger than I am. That means she'd be in the third grade— if she went to school, which she doesn't.

I'll explain later. Promise.

Maddie knows how crazy Mom and Dad can be sometimes. But to be honest, even though she's

WHAT DO YOU WANNA TALK ABOUT THIS MORNING?

ANYTHING. BUT LET'S NOT GIVE AWAY THE WHOLE STORY IN THE FIRST CHAPTER.

younger, Maddie keeps things under control *way* better than I do.

"Everything will be okay, Sammy. Promise."

"But you totally agree that Mom's new idea is ridiculous, right? I could die of embarrassment!"

"I hope not," says Maddie. "I'd miss you. Big-time. And yeah, her plan is a little out there...."

"Maddie, it's so far 'out there' it might as well be on Mars with that robot rover. They could dig up red rocks together!"

Okay, now here's the worst part: My mom told me that this wacko thing she wants me to do is all part of her "most important experiment ever."

Yep. I'm just Mom's poor little guinea pig. She probably put let-tuce leaves in my lunch box.

CHAPTER 2

Mom's "Take a Robot to School Day" idea is so super nutty, she couldn't even say it out loud in front of Genna Zagoren, a girl in my class who has a peanut allergy, which is why my best buddy, Trip, can never eat his lunch at Genna's table. More about Trip later, too. Promise.

Anyhow, it's time to begin Mom's big, *super-important* experiment: me and a walking, talking trash can going to school. Together.

"Just pretend he's your brother" is what my mom says.

"I don't have a brother."

"You do now."

Can you believe this? I can't.

As for the robot? I don't think he's really going to blend in with the other kids in my class except, maybe, on Halloween.

He's already wearing his costume.

"Good morning, Samuel," E says when we're out the front door and on our way up the block to the bus stop. "Lovely weather for matriculating."

"Huh?"

"To matriculate. To enroll or be enrolled in an institution of learning, especially a college or university."

I duck my head and hope nobody can tell it's me walking beside Robo-nerd.

GREAT. MOM'S SENDING ME TO SCHOOL WITH C-3PO.

"We're not going to college," I mumble. "It's just school."

"Excellent. Fabulous. Peachy."

I guess Mom is still working on E's word search program. I can hear all sorts of things whirring as the big bulky thing kind of glides up the sidewalk. The robot chugs his arms back and forth like he's cross-country skiing up the concrete in super-slow motion. Without skis.

I notice that E is lugging an even bigger backpack than I am.

Maybe that's where he keeps his spare batteries.

READ MORE IN

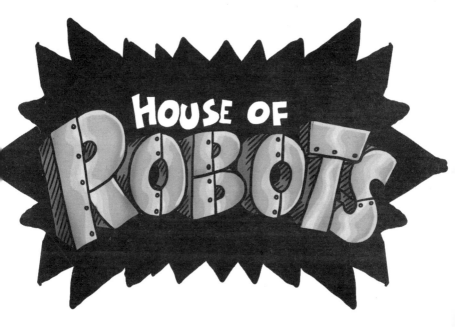

JAMES PATTERSON is the internationally bestselling author of the highly praised Middle School books, *Kenny Wright: Superhero*, *Homeroom Diaries*, and the I Funny, Treasure Hunters, House of Robots, Confessions, Maximum Ride, Witch & Wizard and Daniel X series. James Patterson has been the most borrowed author in UK libraries for the past eight years in a row and his books have sold more than 300 million copies worldwide, making him one of the best-selling authors of all time. He lives in Florida.

CHRIS GRABENSTEIN is a *New York Times* best-selling author who has also collaborated with James Patterson on the I Funny and Treasure Hunters series. He lives in New York City.

JULIANA NEUFELD is an award-winning illustrator whose drawings can be found in books, on album covers, and in nooks and crannies throughout the Internet. She lives in Toronto.